I0764296

Snakes, Butterbeans, & the Discovery of Electricity

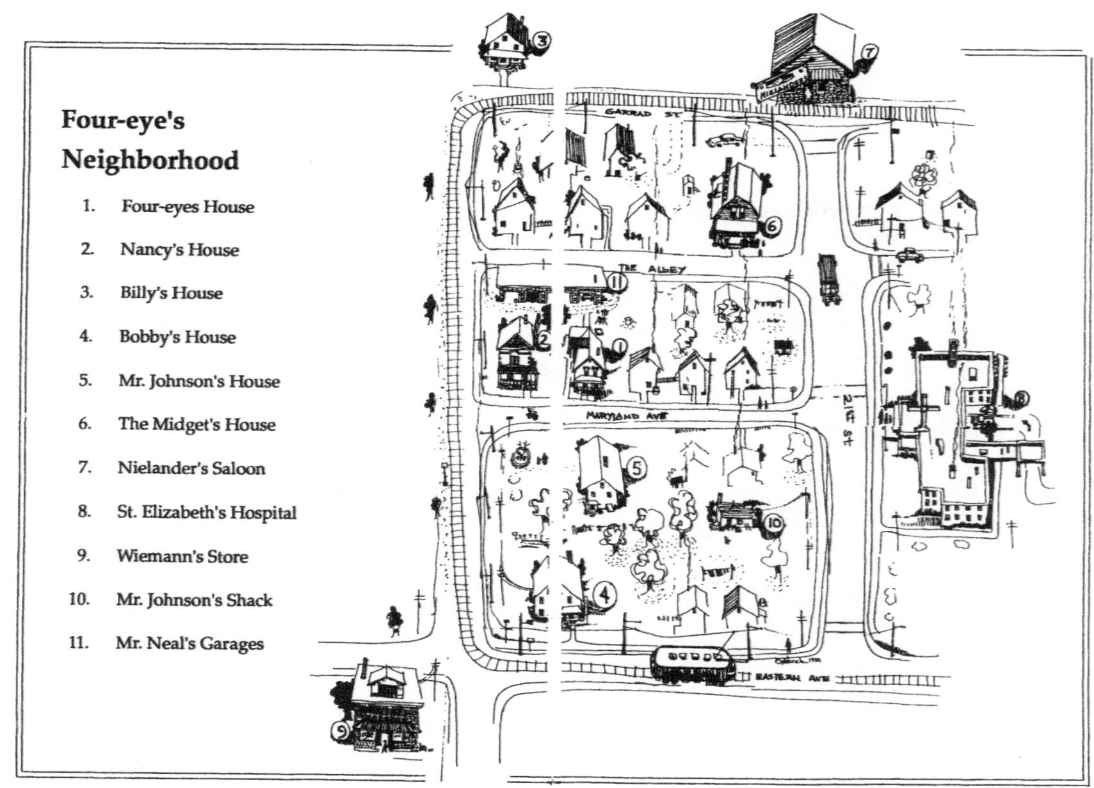

Four-eye's Neighborhood

1. Four-eyes House
2. Nancy's House
3. Billy's House
4. Bobby's House
5. Mr. Johnson's House
6. The Midget's House
7. Nielander's Saloon
8. St. Elizabeth's Hospital
9. Wiemann's Store
10. Mr. Johnson's Shack
11. Mr. Neal's Garages

Snakes, Butterbeans, & the Discovery of Electricity

Stories by

James Ashbrook Perkins

Introduction by
William J. McTaggart

Afterword by
Robie Macauley

Illustrations by
Nelson Oestreich

Mercer University Press
Macon, Georgia

ISBN 0-86554-814-5
MUP/H617

Published in 2003 by

Mercer University Press
6316 Peake Road
Macon, Georgia 31210-3960

∞The paper used in this publication meets the minimum requirements of American National Standard for Information Sciences—Permanence of Paper for Printed Library Materials, ANSI Z39.48-1992.

Publisher's note: No animal was hurt or harmed in any way in the process of the writing or publishing of this book. Any references to animals or animal parts is fiction and does not refer to any real animal, living or dead. The chicken gizzards contained herein are also fictional and is an attempt at humor, and no real chicken gizzards are actually in this book.

Library of Congress Cataloging-in-Publication Data
Perkins, James Ashbrook.
Snakes, butterbeans & the discovery of electricity : stories / by James Ashbrook Perkins ; introduction by William J. McTaggart ; afterword by Robie Macauley ; illustrations by Nelson Oestreich.
p. cm.
ISBN 0-86554-814-5 (alk. paper) — ISBN 0-86554-815-3 (pbk. : alk. paper)
1. Boys—Fiction. 2. Domestic fiction, American. 3. Kentucky—Social life and customs—Fiction. I. Title: Snakes, butterbeans, and the discovery of electricity. II. Title.
PS3566.E69148S65 2003
813'.54–dc21

2003006890

Contents

Acknowledgments

All of these stories appeared in *Snakes, Butterbeans & The Discovery of Electricity*. New Wilmington PA: Dawn Valley Press of Westminster College, 1990.

The following stories, some of them in a different form, appeared in *Billy-the Kid, Chicken Gizzards and Other Tales*. New Wilmington PA: Dawn Valley Press, 1977: "Well, Boys, the Colonel is Dead," "The Great Train Robbery," "Mending Wall," "What's a Friend For?" "Billy and the Demon Rum," "Cinder Hill," "Armageddon," "Billy and the Taft Newspaper," "Gangbusters," "The Gun," "A Real Pickle," "Walter Savage and His Low Moan," "The Bold Raccoon Waits," "Hands Up, We've Got You Covered," "The Last Time I Saw Billy," and "Chicken Gizzards."

"Chicken Gizzards" was reprinted in *Patterns and Themes*. Ed. Judy R. and Glenn C. Rogers. Belmont CA: Wadsworth 1985; 2nd ed. 1988; 3rd ed. 1993, in *The Writer's Workplace*. Ed. Sandra Scarry and John Scarry. New York: Harcourt Brace 1997, in *Westminster College Magazine* (Spring/Summer 1998): 15-16; in *Reading Comprehension*. Ed. Barbara B. Travis. Dubuque: Kendall/Hunt 1996, and in *Keys to Better College English*. Ed. Carol H. Bader and Harley F. Anton. Marlton NJ: Townsend 1996.

"Don't You Know Anything, Boy?" appeared in *Phoenix* Winter 1978 and was reprinted in *Sunrust* (Fall/Winter) 1989–1990.

"Foureyes and the Midgets" appeared in *Sunrust* Fall 1983.

"Making a Mark on the World" was reprinted in *Patterns and Themes*. Ed. Judy R. and Glenn C. Rogers. 4th ed. Belmont CA: Wadsworth 2000.

"Snakes," "The Gun," "The Sting," and "Tippy's Headache," were reprinted in *Sunrust* (Fall/Winter 1989–1990).

"The Homecoming" appeared in *US 1 Worksheets* 22/23 (Spring 1989).

"What's a Friend For?" appeared in *Scrawl* 27.1 (Fall 1874) and was reprinted in *Scrawl*: *50th Anniversary Edition* (March 1989).

"Music Hath Charms" was written at Princeton University in 1987 as a project in a summer seminar on the uses of narrative in history, sponsored jointly by the National Endowment for the Humanities and the East Central Colleges.

"Fireworks," "Making a Mark on the World," "Rats, Killer Turtles, and Naked Fat Men," and "Smelling the Ozone, Up Close and Personal" were written at Yale University in 1989 during a summer seminar led by R. W. B. Lewis on the writings of Robert Penn Warren sponsored by the National Endowment for the Humanities.

For
Jane Allen Perkins
and for
James and Jeffrey
who will always be
Jimbo and Brook
And now for
Joshua and Rory

Foreword

I never planned to be a writer, much less a short story writer. It comes as somewhat of a shock to me that my short story collection *Snakes, Butterbeans & the Discovery of Electricity* is being republished by Mercer University Press some twenty-five years after the first appearance of some of these stories.

When I went to Centre College in 1959 I wanted to be a lawyer and I wanted to be from somewhere exciting like Paris or London or New York rather than from Covington, Kentucky. I certainly didn't want to be like David Madden (author of *Bijou*, *Cassandra Singing*, and *The New Orleans of Possibilities)* who had just published his first novel *The Beautiful Greed* and was teaching at Centre. I heard him read at a compulsory convocation, and his stories reminded me of those my father's family told around the supper table. He did not look like a lawyer, and I avoided him. All this just proves that I had not learned much up to then. Place is important. My father said, "If you know who you are and where you're from, they can't hurt you." He was mostly right. What he forgot to say is that you can hurt yourself if you don't accept who you are and where you're from.

After years at Centre, I began to realize that the education that I had believed was supposed to allow me to escape from my past was instead undermining my desire to do so. The solid liberal arts environment at Centre sent me in search of myself and of my past, and the basically humanitarian faculty loved and supported me without requiring my transformation. The library supplied me with enough law books to allow me to discover that few people on the face of the earth were less apt than I for a study of the law. Those books were dull, but some of the others I found there weren't.

I came away from Centre in 1963 with no clear idea of what I wanted to do, but Centre was important because it gave me four years to discover who I was and where I was from, four years to find out where I left off and the world began. And after those four years, I accepted the facts.

I was well into graduate school at the University of Tennessee on my way to a Ph.D. in American Literature when a student asked me why a poet we were reading did something. I had no idea. The New Criticism I had been taught discouraged speculation about the writer's motives and state of mind. I can honestly say that I started writing poems so I could answer that student's question.

Of course by the time I had written enough poetry to answer the question, that student had graduated and I had taken a job teaching creative writing at Westminster. Since I had never had a creative writing course, I wasn't sure what should happen in one. In those early courses, we read literature, and I gave my students the space to try to discover what they could say. I don't think I harmed anyone too much.

I continued to try to learn this strange craft by sending my work out to magazines to undergo the baffling scrutiny of editors and by attending writer's conferences. For six summers in a row I attended The St. Lawrence/*fiction international* Writers Conference on Upper Tupper Lake near Saranac, New York. I also began reading my poetry on tours to other colleges and universities.

Since the human mind can only endure so much poetry, I told anecdotes between poems. Often books fill the spaces between poems with interesting stories about the process of writing or about where the poem came from. These things I didn't much know myself, so I told funny stories about my family and my childhood.

Nancy James, who taught English with me at Westminster College for years and who had published some of my poetry by then, heard some of these anecdotes and said to me "You ought to put out a collection of short stories." That led to *Billy-the-Kid*,

Chicken Gizzards and Other Tales (my first collection) and eventually to *Snakes, Butterbeans & the Discovery of Electricity*, a volume that reprinted the stories in the first volume and added about a dozen new ones.

Who I am is largely dependent on where I am from. And these stories are the result of bringing specific places to mind. Since my writing depends more on dialogue than description, the places in the stories may remain vague to the reader. Since I cannot reproduce my memories or enclose copies of the snapshots that are spread out here on my desk, I have asked Nelson Oestreich to create maps of some of the places in my childhood for this volume.

My backyard, my neighborhood, the midgets' house, the hollyhocks, the car tracks, Nielander's Saloon: all of these places are woven into the fabric of my normal happy childhood. It was a childhood like yours, played out in a time before malls, when the cookies in the jar were always homemade. Yes, place is important.

Sometime along the way I started sending stories out to magazines, so by the time my first collection of stories went out of print I had an acceptable number of stories published in magazines.

One of the title stories in the first collection, "Chicken Gizzards," has proven quite popular. It has really taken on a life of its own. In 1985 Glenn Rogers, a friend from my undergraduate days at Centre College in Kentucky, asked if he could include "Chicken Gizzards" in a developmental reader he and his wife Judy were preparing. He liked the story because it was funny and especially because when he applied a reading level analysis to it, the story measured at about eighth grade reading level. What can I say? I used nearly every word I know; I used some of them twice.

Those kind folks also reprinted my story in the second and the third edition of their *Patterns and Themes*. I was right there in the table of contents between Garrison Keillor and Art Buchwald. That same story has now appeared in three other reading textbooks. A number of things about all this amuse me. I am tickled by the assumption, stated by the various editors in their introductions, that the story is completely true, that I am merely recounting events from my childhood. If that were true, I wouldn't be a fiction writer at all. I would be just another memoirist, and we have enough of those just now.

It is true that the men in my family, for reasons I could never understand, all liked chicken gizzards. It is also true that a woman Bible salesman's panties fell down around her ankles while she was standing on the front porch trying to sell my uncle a Bible. The rest, well, I sort of made the rest up.

I am also amused and a bit baffled by the questions the editors ask at the end of the story. For example, "Daddy, Pap, and Uncle Eddie have various tricks for getting the gizzard. List them in the order in which they occur in the sketch. Why does the author use this order?" I really can't answer this question. I haven't a clue. This inability worried me for a while. Then I realized that I don't analyze my stories. I already discovered everything I wanted to know about these stories while I was writing them.

When I read stories, and I read a lot of stories, I read Bobbie Ann Mason, Lee Smith, Eudora Welty, William Faulkner, Robert Drake, David Madden, and Lewis Nordan. I suppose I read these stories with my critical hat on. I know I am able to answer questions about them and write critical articles about them. My own stories I just write to find out what is going to happen to all these very strange people whose voices are in my head. I write them, simply to tell stories like the ones I heard around the dinner table when I was growing up. I write them and then I put them out somewhere and hope that folks will enjoy them. With the support of Mercer University Press (especially Marc A. Jolley, Kevin C. Manus, and Marsha Luttrell) I am doing that again. I hope you will enjoy all of these.

James A. Perkins
New Wilmington 2002

Introduction

When I was a boy growing up back in the 1940s, one of the treats in my life was the arrival of my Aunt Marion. Every few weeks, she would come from the Western Pennsylvania School for the Deaf to spend a weekend with my grandmother.

We anticipated these visits mostly because Aunt Marion would open her cheap suitcase and hand over all the motion picture magazines she had saved for us. My cousins Ruth and Helen would pore through the fan magazines looking for pictures in gaudy colors of their favorites, Jeanne Crain, and Lana Turner and Humphrey Bogart and Cary Grant, while I was regularly disappointed by the dearth of similar photographs of my favorites, Gene Autry and Edward G. Robinson. My cousins would carefully cut out their latest finds and pin them over the wallpaper of the bedroom they shared, while I'd walk next door to my house, disappointed again. It was tough being eight years old and being in love with a cowboy and gangster who weren't considered glamorous enough to be photographed.

Anyway, to get back to Aunt Marion: she was a deaf mute. There was no question about her being deaf, but I never did understand the mute part, since she had a voice and had learned to talk *almost* intelligibly. Of course, all the members of the family figured that if they shouted loudly enough, Aunt Marion would *hear* them, which was nonsense, but nevertheless made for extremely loud and raucous Sunday dinners.

My aunt loved the movies. I suppose she enjoyed them more than we did, since we could *hear* what the actors said, thus getting a literal interpretation of the plot and all the rest of that stuff. But lucky Aunt Marion could pretty much make up her own stories from the few visual elements the screen provided for her, which meant that in some ways, she never saw a movie she didn't like.

When I think of Aunt Marion, I think of the way she'd laugh loudly in bed at night or while sitting on my grandmother's porch glider, laughing hours later at something funny she had just remembered. She couldn't hear her own laugh, so it was the most spontaneous and unaffected laugh I've ever heard. She would simply let out with a kind of breathless, giggly roar, laughing because it felt good, even though in that Lucille Ball head of hers, all she could feel was the silence and the shaking.

I also remember how much fun it was to "listen" to her reading a book. I'd be seated on the porch steps, there among the geraniums, snapping beans for Grandma, while Grandma herself was out in the backyard removing a chicken from its head with her trusty axe, and my Uncle Dugald would be at the Large Hotel loading up on Fort Pitt beer, and Helen would be in the sitting room tuned to the radio and sewing clothes for her doll, while Ruth was shinnying up trees somewhere watching the sky for airplanes. And I'd sit there checking out Aunt Marion and waiting with almost painful anticipation for that moment when she'd read something funny and then would laugh so long and hard that her eyes would overflow with tears while she fumbled around in her dress pockets searching for her handkerchief to stem the tide.

All of which bring me to the wonderful book you now hold in your hand—*Snakes, Butterbeans, & the Discovery of Electricity* by James Ashbrook Perkins.

Here are thirty-three wonderful tales about Bobby and Billy and James. Though these tales do not take place on the country road where I grew up, there is within every sentence a feeling of warm nostalgia, innocence recaptured—not only the innocence of what seemed a more innocent time, but the innocence of youth and the innocence of truth. These stories feel as if they've been around forever, and we are *all* lucky that Jim finally got around to writing them down.

I'm not going to tell you about them. I'm just going to allow you the pleasure of reading them. And then reading them again.

You'll love them. Every one of them.

I'm going to send a copy to my Aunt Marion. She'll love them, too. She'll probably laugh her head off. I just hope she finds hers handkerchief in time so the pages of the book don't get all splashed up.

Enjoy.

W. J. McTaggart

Well, Boys, the Colonel Is Dead

Wednesday

Nothing ever happened in Brooksville on Wednesday afternoon anyway, and by mid-August the crops were laid by, so the men just hung around town and talked about how bad the weather was and what prices the tobacco would bring. The older men sat in the sun on the benches outside the courthouse chewing Redman and shaving away at white pine sticks with their Barlows, while the younger men stood across the street on the wide, covered front gallery at Williams' General Store, chewing Redman with their fingers laced in the straps of their bib overalls. So when Curley Beckett ran down the broken concrete front steps of the courthouse and cut across the side yard to Doc Green's house, the whittlers paused; and when five minutes later Curley came back dragging Doc Green, who, still wearing a pair of green plaid house slippers, was running sort of sideways trying to put on his black suit coat without dropping his bag, a buzz of conversation broke out.

"What's up, Curley?"

"Something happen?"

"Who's sick?"

Curley didn't answer, didn't slow down, and Doc Green just succeeded in getting his coat on as Curley shoved him through the door.

By the time the older men had returned to their pine sticks, a vanguard of younger men from Williams' had crossed the street and come up the walk.

"Afternoon, Mr. McDivot. What's going on?"

"No idea, McBride. Curley just ran out and got the Doc and run back in."

"What did Curley say?"

"Nothing. Not a word."

"Ain't like Curley. You ever know him to pass up a chance to bend a man's ear?"

A new black Dodge sedan swerved to a stop at the curb, and Mrs. R. C. Jorgansen III, wife of the mayor, jumped from behind the wheel and ran up the courthouse walk. The knot of men at the steps parted to let her pass.

"Afternoon, Miz Jorgansen."

"Afternoon, Mr. McDivot."

"What is a-goin'. . ." McDivot didn't bother to finish his question because the lady was already through the door.

About two-thirty Curley Beckett came out. The crowd of men had grown. In fact, there was no one left on Williams' gallery.

"Well, boys, the Colonel is dead."

Curley had served in World War I with "the Colonel," as he was called. We had all read in the paper about his heroic exploits, but to the rest of us he was just R. C. Jorgansen III of Jorgansen's Seed and Feed. At least he was until he became mayor.

"Dead? R. C. dead?"

"That's right. Doc Green's up there now signing the papers. I was down the hall trying to figure out what the hell that new limited doe hunting law was going to mean, and I heard this big thud. I run up the hall, and there was R. C. flat on the floor, pale as store-bought flour. I run out and got Doc Green..."

"I saw you, Curley. By God! You were making tracks."

"Well, Doc looked at R. C. and told me to call his wife. He said there wasn't nothing he could do."

"When's the funeral, Curley?"

"Don't know for sure, but it won't do to keep him long in this hot weather. I'd say Friday. Doc's calling Whiteside."

"Gawd, they's going be more people to that buryin' than come to see Brother Barnstaple's faith healing."

"Don't you just know it. It will be the biggest thing in this town since the spur line came."

Thursday

It was big. Mrs. R. C. Jorgansen III was nigh wore out answering the door and carrying casseroles into the kitchen.

"Can't stay, Birdie. I just wanted you to know we're thinking about you. This is some of the spinach souffle that Aunt Rose Louise used to make for the Methodist potluck supper."

"Thank you, Mrs. Brown. How on earth did you ever get that recipe? I offered her my banana-nut-honey bread for it, and she acted like I'd tried to steal something."

"Well, you know how peculiar Aunt Rose Louise was, rest her soul. We'll see you this afternoon."

"Thank you, dear."

It was a wonder that the ladies didn't walk over each other carrying food up to the Jorgansen's door all morning Thursday.

About noon, Mr. Thurston Ross Whiteside drove up to the Jorgansen home in that Packard hearse with the right front fender still bent from where Only Johnson rammed it with his Ford truck when Turkey Neck (that's what everybody called Mr. Ross behind his back) ran the stop sign at the crossroads out near Pig Misery. (Turkey Neck said he had his siren on and Only said he didn't. Miz T. R. Curtis, who was in the back of the hearse, on her way to the hospital, wasn't any good as a witness 'cause when the crash happened she up and had her seventh child, Sarah Lee Louise, right there in the intersection.)

Mr. Ross and Bernard brought the coffin in and set it on two sawhorses with a black cloth draped over them in the parlor. He said that the viewing would be easier to handle in the dining room because it had two doors, but Miz Jorgansen insisted that he put R. C. in the parlor. It took Turkey Neck and Bernard about an hour to get all the flowers arranged and that scrim laid over the open coffin to keep the flies off.

Folks started arriving about half past three for the viewing. By seven no one had left and most everybody else had come, and it was easy to see that Mr. Ross knew his rooms. The Jorgansen's parlor was half full of coffin and flowers and clear full of sad, sweaty people, which made it a bit over-full. Just after Clevenger Williams, founder and retired manager of Williams' General Store, reminded the assemblage in the proper mournful tones of how, one summer when he was home from college, R. C. had passed out cold trying to keep up with Big Smokey driving spikes when the spur line was put in, Miss Ida Faye Bossier, Miz Jorgansen's maid sister from Cincinnati, her only living relative, who had come up to Maysville on a packet boat to visit for the summer, fainted dead away.

When Curley Beckett and old Mr. Williams got her out into the yard where the children were catching fireflies and trying to be as restrained as the occasion demanded, several cigar-smoking men with their coats flung over their shoulder offered help.

"That heat finally got one of 'em, eh Curley?"

"You bet. That room smells like of them French cat houses with all that hot flesh and them flowers."

Mr. Williams got some water from the pump and gave it to Miss Ida, who revived from the heat of the parlor only to nearly succumb to the exhaled cigar smoke of her attendant saviors.

The viewing went on till past ten o'clock, with the ladies of the VFW helping Birdie Jorgansen, who just refused to leave her kitchen, put out a buffet for that crowd. And it was a crowd. Sheriff Elwood Trube said, and he was quoted in the paper the next week, "There ain't been a crowd like that in this town since the high school team came in second at the State Basketball Tournament." Crowd or not, they barely made a dent in the food folks had been packing into the Jorgansen's kitchen all morning.

After the viewing, Turkey Neck took a look at the body and told Miz Jorgansen that due to the extreme weather they were going to have to remove the body and bring it back the next morning for the funeral. Miz Jorgansen thought, and said so later to Miz Minnie Williams, young Mr. Clevenger Willimas' cute little wife from Bath County, that Mr. Ross was going to take the body back to Whiteside's for the evening. But Turkey Neck knew the signs. He could see the puffiness coming into R. C.'s face, and he knew that the body was getting ripe in all that heat, so he paid Milton Travis, the night watchman, a dollar and slipped R. C. into the big locker down at the Farmer's Cooperative Freezer Plant.

Friday

It was a good idea and probably nobody would have ever known if Miz Jorgansen hadn't gotten up nervous on Friday. She decided to settle herself down by making a big batch of her county-fair-blue-ribbon-winning sausage balls and then discovered that she didn't have any sausage. Birdie got to the Freezer Plant just as Colston Renfro was opening up. She pulled open the big locker door, and there stood R. C. in his best blue suit with ice hanging off his moustache. It took Doc Green better than an hour to get her settled down, but later, she said Mr. Ross had probably done the right thing, considering the weather.

The service itself was uneventful except for the steady drip of water from R. C. thawing out in that heat, and then everybody lined up behind Turkey Neck and headed out toward Linwood to the cemetery. They were about a mile out of town when the new volunteer fire department steam whistle, which run off a pipe from Mr. Ling-Sam's hand laundry, went off. Besides owning the funeral home and running the ambulance service, Turkey Neck was the chief of the volunteer fire company. Funeral or no funeral, he turned on his siren and flashing red light that he bought after Only Johnson dented the front fender, spun that Packard hearse around, and headed toward the smoke.

Most everybody in the funeral line was a volunteer, so they all turned around and followed the hearse, and the one that weren't volunteers had no place to go, so they followed too. As they passed through town, they added the pumper truck to the head of the line and all wound up at Lum Waystead's machinery shed. It was smoldering in the loft, but it hadn't got a good start yet. Lum got out of his car and came running up to the door.

"Goldernit. My keys are in my work pants. We're going to have to bust that door in. My new Oliver and that cultivator are in there."

"Get the keys, Lum," Turkey Neck shouted.

"No time, Mr. Ross. Them keys are at the house. Damn thing would burn down 'fore I could get back."

Turkey Neck got some of the boys to play one hose on the roof and another into the loft through the ventilators while he sent Leon Thompson back to the truck for an axe. Lum just shook his head.

"Axe ain't going to take that door down, not today, anyways. We're going to have to bust it down."

"OK, boys," yelled Turkey Neck, "get that four-by-four over by the fence and ram this here door down."

They ran at the door a half a dozen times till finally Leon Thompson said, "It's no good, Mr. Ross, we need something heavier."

Turkey Neck stood there in the smoke and water with the fire hat doing little to protect his white shirt and black suit. Suddenly he ran to the back of the hearse.

"Come on, boys. Give me a hand."

"What are you goin' to do, Mr. Ross?"

"I'm going to use this coffin to bust down that door."

"Ain't you better ask Miz Jorgansen?"

Turkey Neck's business sense got the better of his civic emotionalism, and he requested the widow's permission to use her late husband's remains for a battering ram. She consented, but only if the pallbearers could do the job. That almost ruined it.

K. L. Jorgansen, R. C.'s younger brother who lived over in Maryland, was a pallbearer, but he wasn't a member of the volunteer fire company. Finally, although there are some who hold it against him still, Turkey Neck said that it would just have to be that way because that was what the widow said.

Now that, I want to tell you, was a sight—those six men, in the only rented morning coats that the town had ever seen, running headlong with R. C.'s coffin smack into that shed door. Well, it worked. That door gave way enough to peel those men right off those coffin rails and send that coffin flying into the burning building.

Lum Waystead ran past the pallbearers, who were pushing the doors open wider. By the time Turkey Neck could get inside to look for the coffin, Lum had wedged the clutch down on the Oliver and was dragging a tow chain out the door. It wasn't enough to reach any of the cars, so the six pallbearers grabbed it and pulled the Oliver out of the shed.

"In here, boys," Turkey Neck yelled. "Put the hose on that straw right here."

The small straw fire was quickly extinguished, and the pallbearers lifted the slightly singed coffin from the smoldering remains.

It took about an hour to put the fire out completely. Then, Turkey Neck put his chief's hat back on the pumper and headed out for the cemetery with R. C. in the coffin in the back once again.

At the graveside, the Reverend Glass made a little speech about how we all knew that R. C. had never missed a fire while he was alive and how we all prayed that he had seen his very last one now that he was dead. Lots of folks thought it was a nice talk, but a lot of others didn't care for it one bit, and the Presbyterian Church was over two years getting themselves a new minister. Folks came back to the Jorgansen's place after the burying, the way they always do to console the widow, but they just sat around trying to pull themselves together. Birdie and the girls from the VFW carried around trays of cold ham and a jillion kinds of salads and vegetables, but hardly anybody ate anything. They just sat around asking, "Was there ever such a day?"

Saturday

Well, there was such a day, the very next day. Saturday morning at about ten, Mr. Paul Luckett, P. V. Luckett's boy, the lawyer, read R. C.'s last will and testament over at the Jorgansen's place. About eleven, Curley Beckett and Turkey Neck showed up in that Packard hearse and picked up young Mr. Paul and Miz Jorgansen. By twelve, when the once-a-day train pulled into the station on the spur line, most of the town knew and was there to see them put that beat-up, burned coffin on the mail car and see Miz Jorgansen and Miss Ida get on the pullman. It seems that the "Colonel" business was right strong, 'cause the only thing R. C. requested in his will was that, in the light of his service to his country, they was to bury him at the National Military Cemetery in Arlington, Virginia.

Don't You Know Anything, Boy?

I stood on the back solarium, looking through the frost lacework on the windows and tucking a heavy sweater into my pants.

"Hurry, lazybones. Your father went to the barn nearly half an hour ago."

"Yes'm."

"You remember last Tuesday, don't you?"

"Yes'm."

Oh yes, I remembered. I remembered Daddy saying, "Why, son?"

"It's just too cold. I didn't want to."

"Well. I told you to, didn't I?"

"Yes, sir."

"When I tell you to do something, I expect you to do it. Do you understand?"

"Yes, sir."

"Well. Just to impress it on your memory, I want you to come out to the garage with me."

"Yes, sir."

The garage was where my father impressed things on me. And not just on my memory either.

My mother's voice broke my reverie.

"I want you to have those chickens done before he gets back. Don't forget the keys."

"Yes'm," I said again and grabbed my big hunting parka from its nail by the door. I slapped the right shell pocket and heard the keys rattle.

We had lots of chickens. "More chickens," as Daddy said, "than a sane man would want." We hatched out a couple of thousand every spring. A few would drown in the brooder house. A few of the dumb ones would get carried off by owls and hawks. The rest we had to feed and look after until the day when the paper said the price was about right, and Daddy announced that Armageddon was about to commence. Anyway, we had lots of chickens, and Daddy never minded the few that we lost to the hawks and owls. But when it appeared that the hawks and owls were opening the chicken house door and carrying off the hens in feed sacks, we got a lock.

It was cold. The snow crunched and squeaked under my boots as I walked through the yard to the chicken house. When I lifted the lock with my right hand, the cold knifed through the brown cotton palm of my Red Rider gloves. After several attempts, I realized that the lock was frozen.

"Well. Did you get the chickens done?"

"No, sir. I couldn't. The lock's froze."

"Well. Lick it. Don't you know anything, boy? Go on. I'll be there as soon as I get my boots back on."

"Yes, sir."

It began as a very light green, like snow-blanketed ice on the creek with dark water trickling beneath it. It was cold and painful. I could not shut my mouth. It became lighter and lighter till it was a cry of white, and I could not tell whether it was cold or hot. I knew that I was sobbing and screaming, but all I could hear was the awful whiteness and through it a deeper sound.

"You damn fool. You damn little fool. Don't you know anything, boy? Stick your tongue on a frozen lock. Now this is going to hurt," he said as he swung his big leg and swept my feet out from under me. I fell.

It was no longer white. It was red, a high-pitched, wailing red. The tip of my tongue whitened quickly on a swinging lock above me, and the snow beneath my face reddened.

"You get to the house. I'll do the chickens."

Finally the bleeding stopped, and I sat at the big blue table in the middle of the kitchen drinking warm milk through a straw.

"Too bad you hurt your tongue, son. I fixed this sausage and mush special for you."

"Hell," said my father, pausing with a forkful of mush halfway to his mouth, "the boy's got to learn not to do everything he's told."

Bully and the Demon Rum

Winter evenings, after the chores were done and the dinner dishes were put away, my mother read to me one chapter a night of Laura Ingles Wilder's *Farmer Boy* in front of the fire while the wind rattled against clap siding and whistled in the chimney. Each night I climbed the cold winding stair to the sleeping loft over the kitchen and crawled under the down comforter to dream of Almonzo. In the spring, inspired by Almonzo's thrift, I took my Christmas money (saved by the hardest, through a long winter of window-shopping) and bought two pigs at the Walton livestock auction. They were just-weaned Hampshires, and through the summer I watched them grow along with the field corn, the garden, and the robins nesting just outside the kitchen window.

When fall came and the first hard freeze, my father began to talk about killing the hogs. It was not something I ever really got used to, but growing up on a small farm made death no stranger. On the spring mornings I would go over to the brooder house and find several of the newly hatched chicks drowned, and autumn evenings I would see owls wheeling over the stubble of the corn fields waiting for mice. And after the first hard freeze there was a silence in the twilight that told me that the crickets were gone. We slaughtered three of my father's hogs, but my two were sold at auction along with the rest of father's to a local meat packer, and again I put the money by.

The next spring I bought two calves at the auction. They were very young, a Hereford heifer and a Brown Swiss bull, and we had to feed them from a nipple bucket. After a few weeks I taught the heifer to drink from a bucket, but that fool bull never learned. Again and again he snorted and snuffed and nearly drowned, but he never learned to drink.

After tossing hay into the mow one evening, I dropped down into the calf pen and found "Bully" lying on his side moaning and snorting.

I had never been in a liquor store before, but the rows and rows of bottles of varied colored liquid made me think of svelte, well-dressed ladies I had seen in the whisky ads.

"I'd like a fifth of bourbon," my father told the clerk.

"What brand?"

"It doesn't matter. It's for a calf. Got pneumonia. The vet said to give it warm whiskey and water."

"How 'bout this Mattingly and Moore? My boss says it isn't fit for humans."

"That'll be fine."

We fed Bully the warm whiskey and water with the nipple pail. He was so weak he didn't drink much at all. That night at supper my mother said that the calf would die because it drank the whiskey, and I climbed into the loft and pulled the covers up to my chin. For a long time I lay there watching the moonlight shadows of the maple tree playing on the walls, figuring out what the changing shapes could be. Then I prayed.

The next morning I went straight to the calf pen. Bully was dead. He was lying on his side with his neck twisted back and his legs already stiff.

Summer faded into autumn and Red, the heifer, grew. Sometimes standing in the kitchen at night watching mother get supper, I would look up at the half-empty whiskey bottle on the top shelf and remember the man who had come with a truck and pulled Bully into the back of it with a winch. But usually, after the corn was laid by, I swam in the pond or played on the grapevines till the coming cold drove me back to the hearthside and books.

One evening my father came in from the barn, took his boots off in the mudroom, walked into the kitchen, and took the whiskey bottle from the shelf.

"Getting a sore throat. Warm some water. I think I'll have a toddy before supper."

Mother said nothing, and throughout the evening father "freshened" his drink until, by the time I climbed the winding stairs, there was only a fourth of the amber liquid in the bottle on the top shelf.

In the chill of the loft I lay with the comforter resting under my chin. The moonlight through the maple tree cast shadows on the walls, and I lay there seeing only the shadows and thinking of how foolish I had been ever to imagine that they were Spanish galleons, or clouds, or the sea. Then, wishing I could pray, I cried until I fell to sleep.

When I came down the stairs into the cold slanting light of the kitchen the next morning I found my father sitting at the table behind an enormous pile of pancakes.

"Good morning, son. Sleep well?"

"Uh, yes sir."

Armageddon

Daddy put the phone down and walked to his chair near the stove. Mother filled his plate again with fried apples and pork chops and said, "Well?" That was her all-purpose word—interrogative, interjection, or imperative, depending on the tone of her voice. This time it was clearly a question.

"Ed says he and Esther'll be glad to help with the chickens and stay for supper too. It's a good thing because I got the wine this afternoon."

"Do you think he suspects anything?"

"No. He probably hasn't remembered it yet himself."

"Well," she said again, and this time it had the resigned quality of a woman who had, herself, known a man who would forget his own wife's birthday. We continued to eat in silence till Daddy said, "Son. You better turn in early tonight. Tomorrow's going to be Armageddon around here. There'll be lots of work for you to do."

Armageddon, as Daddy called it, was the day we killed chickens—not just a few chickens for the freezer, but more than five hundred chickens for sale to the local locker plant. I finished my pie and milk, said my goodnights, and then marched up the winding stairs to the sleeping loft to dream of the coming slaughter.

My aunt and uncle came in the backdoor just as I was swallowing the last bite of my fifth plate of pancakes.

"Good morning, y'all. How are you today, gimlet-butt?"

"I'm fine, Uncle Eddie."

"Son, if you're finished eating, go get the hamper and bring the first batch to the chopping block."

We had ourselves a regular assembly line Armageddon. I brought the hens out of the chicken house in a hamper. Daddy grabbed them by the head with his left hand and pulled their necks over the chopping block while I held their bodies. Then the wide-blade hatchet in his right hand came down in a neat short stroke. He never had to tell me to let go. There was an explosion of flopping, fluttering, diving blood and feathers. Even after I'd seen a thousand chickens die, I never got used to the strange sounds their bodies made as they flopped around the yard. Uncle Eddie thought using a hatchet was a waste of time. He just reached down and grabbed a hen by the head, snapped his arm like a buggy whip, and sent the headless hen sailing across the yard.

After the hens quit thrashing around, I picked them up and piled them by the big iron kettle that was boiling on the driveway. There Daddy held the hens by their legs, dipped them into the scalding water, and then passed them to Uncle Eddie, who plucked them clean while he kept me entranced with some wild tale or other.

"Seeing all these chicken heads laying around reminds me of the geeks we'd keep at the freak tent when I was with the carnival."

"What's a geek, Uncle Eddie?"

"The boy wants to know what a geek is," said Uncle Eddie.

"Well, you brought it up; you tell him," said Daddy, handing Uncle Eddie another scalded chicken.

"Well, gimlet-butt. Let's see here. Geeks. Well, geeks were old men we kept around the carnival. Yep. That's what geeks were."

"What did they have to do with chicken heads?"

"Well. You see. Chicken heads. Are you sure you want him to hear this?"

"Go ahead and tell it. But keep pulling the feathers off them birds. They's a lot more where those came from."

"OK kid. Geeks. Whenever we could, we'd pick up a wino and keep him off the sauce till he started shakin' and seein' things. Then we'd give him a chicken and razor blade and tell him we'd give him a gallon of Richard's Wild Irish Rose if he'd do the geek show for us."

"What did he have to do?"

"Ah, you don't want to know about that, gimlet-butt. We're done with this batch anyway. Go to the hen house and fetch us some more."

Three times I crossed the yard with a full hamper of hens and helped dispatch them, but the story did not proceed. Finally, when I set the hamper down after my fourth trip, I said, "Come on. Finish telling me about the geeks."

"Well," said Eddie as he snaked his arm out and snapped a headless hen into an arc across the backyard, "I don't remember where I was."

"You were just about to tell me what the winos had to do in the geek show."

"Well. All the wino had to do at first was hold the chicken's head in his mouth and on the sly cut it off with the razor blade so it looked to the crowd like he'd bitten it off. Of course, after a few shows we'd pull him off the sauce again and take the razor blade away."

"You mean..."

"Yep. We made them bite the heads right off. Sometimes, if we found ourselves a good geek, we could make them do rats and snakes."

Finally, after we had spent a whole day killing and scalding and plucking and gutting, and Mother and Aunt Esther had spent the day cutting up, 635 chickens lay in plastic bags in the freezer ready to be sold at the local locker plant. We sat down to a big roast beef dinner. We were so tired that when Daddy started cutting the thick slices of rare beef, he didn't even make his usual joke about which one of us would get the gizzard. We'd all seen enough of gizzards for a while.

When Daddy had everyone served, Mother popped out of the kitchen with a fresh pan of rolls in one hand and a bottle of wine in the other.

"Happy birthday!" she and Daddy shouted.

"Oh, shit," said Uncle Eddie. "I forgot again."

"That's all right, dear," said Aunt Esther, smiling. "You haven't remembered my birthday in the last ten years."

"Who wants some wine?" asked Mother. "Son, would you like some? This is a special occasion. Your aunt's only going to be thirty once."

"That's for sure and it ain't likely to be this year."

"You'd better watch it, Mister. You're in enough trouble already for forgetting my birthday. Don't add to your problems."

"Hush, you two. This is supposed to be a party. Do you want some wine, son?"

"No'm."

"Son," said my Daddy, "you're getting older now. If you would like a glass of wine, I think it would be all right. Do you understand?"

"Yes, sir."

"Do you want a glass of wine?"

"No, sir. I don't want to grow up to be no geek."

"Well," said Mother in a tone that suggested that she had been left out of part of the story.

The Bold Raccoon Waits

"Chore-time, lazybones."

Mother's voice drifted up the twisting stairs to the sleeping loft and down into the featherbed where my warm dream fought it and tried to fit it in before finally fading out. The thin eastern light looked strange as I swung my body out of bed. My foot touched the floor, and I knew why. Cold! The sun was coming up in a haze, and there was frost covering the small window. Even the bearskin rug held no warmth. I dug my toe into the hole behind the bear's left eye where one shot from great granddaddy's muzzle loader had entered and forever made bears a myth in Bracken County. I shivered, dressed quickly, and bounded downstairs to stand in the small kitchen, which was always warm with breakfast biscuits baking.

"Here's some cocoa...you'd better get a move on. Your father's already at the barn."

It was more than a frost. The grass crunched when I stepped, the way a hard-crusted hunting snow around Thanksgiving might, and I couldn't crack the ice in the wagon ruts with my boot heel. I slid open the big barn door and climbed to the top of the haymow. Up near the barn roof, it was warm as if the hay somehow retained the summer sun in which it had grown. Below I could hear the steady squirt of the milk against the side of the pail. I forked the hayracks full of timothy and clover and then swung down into the lamplit stalls.

"This is the earliest hard freeze I can remember. After you clean out the stalls, son, you better take the axe and go break out the spring."

Steam rose from the manure that I shoveled into the pile at the edge of the barn lot.

"I'll have to see MacEdwards to see if he wants to start killing hogs. He may, but I don't think this weather will hold. We can probably go hunting today. How would that be, son?"

"Great."

I picked up the axe and headed for the spring. A dry snow had begun while I worked in the barn, and as it blew into the frozen grass, it sounded like sand tossed against a window. If the snow kept up, there would be good tracking weather. A rabbit started from almost under my feet and headed for the ridge. I raised the axe, aimed it, leading just enough, and slowly squeezed the cold axe head with my index finger the way Daddy and Uncle Eddie showed me when they let me shoot at tin cans as a reward for walking soaked to the skin and cold as Christmas, carrying a gun so big it would have torn me in half if I'd ever seen anything to shoot at. I had almost stepped on that rabbit. It had been sitting close; the weather was probably as cold as the day Uncle Eddie caught one sitting so tight that he cracked it in the head with his gun butt. Daddy said they couldn't eat it 'cause they didn't know if it was sick or not. Said Eddie should have kicked it in the ass and then shot it when it ran.

As I came down to the spring, I heard a scraping noise like something dragged quickly past the sunken barrel that formed the spring head. I thought, "snake," then laughed at my fear. No snake would be sunning itself beside a frozen spring. In the deep shadow of the spring head I saw it; a big coon. I stood still to let him know that I wasn't here to harm him, but he made no move to go. I stepped up to the spring pool, and the coon put his forepaws up on the barrel and stared over them through his mask.

The spring pool was frozen hard, and my first axe swing wasn't true. The head glanced off the ice and sent a ringing clatter into the frozen trees. The coon did not blink. Slowly the black ice whitened as my axe released the dark green water. I stood watching the coon as the wind-driven snow disappeared, shard by shard, into the icy water.

The big coon knew no fear past his own need. He stepped stately from his cover by the spring head and stood next to me cupping the cold water into his mouth. Then he walked unhurried to the edge of the buckberry thicket, turned, and was gone.

The stalls were dark again as I passed the barn. I set the axe inside and slid the great door shut once more. On the back porch, I stomped the snow from my boots, and went in to the smell of sausage, mush, and coffee.

"I called MacEdwards, son. He says he's afraid of this weather."

"This would be fine weather for you to clean out the fruit cellar."

"Woman, it's too cold for a man to be clawin' about underground in the dark."

"Just a suggestion. Seems like time's hanging heavy on your hands. Son, you want more sausage?"

"Yes'm. More mush too, if there is any."

"There's plenty. When I saw that cold weather this morning, I knew I'd be cooking a hunter's breakfast. You all eat up now and go on and enjoy yourselves, you hear?"

"What about it, son? I saw some good-sized coon tracks over by the spring the other day."

"I think I'll work on the fruit cellar."

Oestreich
1990

Snakes

I was never really afraid of snakes. I just had a sincere respect for them. I knew they got Adam and Eve in a mess of trouble, and I could usually get in a mess of trouble all by myself.

Surprisingly, my mother did not mind snakes, either. Once when she was a girl, the boy who sat behind her in school, and who tormented her constantly, stuck her pigtail in his inkwell. Mother had to go home early to wash the ink out of her hair. A few days later, on her way to school, she found a little garter snake. She caught it, put it in her lunch pail, and went on to school, where she slid the snake into her tormentor's desk. When he opened his desk to get his books, people heard his screams all the way to the blacksmith's shop. And he had to leave school early to change his clothes.

My daddy's attitude toward snakes operated in direct proportion to their distance from the hen house. A snake out in the yard or in the barn was fine. "Snakes kill mice, son. They're a farmer's friend." But a snake around the hen house was a different snake. "Snakes suck eggs, son. A farmer can't have snakes around his hen house."

Then there was my Uncle Eddie, who told stories about how, when he was a roustabout with the carnival, they'd get winos to bite the heads off snakes in what he called the Geek Show.

Our neighbor McBee was the source of most of my information about snakes, the source of most of my knowledge of folklore in general. McBee didn't think there were any good snakes no matter where the hen house was. It was McBee who told me that if you kill a snake, it will not die until sundown. And he warned me not to cut a snake into pieces and leave the pieces together, because the fragments will unite and crawl away.

The word "crawl" had a lot to do with how I felt toward snakes. They were so sneaky. I seldom really saw one. I saw some quick movement out of the corner of my eye, a ripple in the grass, or a tail whipping off a rock. The ones I saw out of the side of my eye made me worry about the ones that were behind me.

Water snakes were the worst. I knew that the water snakes in Kentucky weren't poisonous, but the murky creek water was scary enough without thinking about turtles or snakes.

Nevertheless, snakes fascinated me. I read all I could about them in the school library. And I loved to spend hours in the reptile house in the Cincinnati Zoo, staring through the thick glass at timber rattlers, black mambas, cobras, water moccasins, and coral snakes. I liked to look at them through the glass. I was never fond of meeting them in the wild.

Mostly I ran into snakes in our cornfield while we were hoeing to give the young corn a fighting chance against the weeds. Hognose snakes were funny. When I came upon one of those, if it didn't have time to slip away it would roll belly up and play dead like a possum. I knew Hognoses were harmless, so I left them alone. Spreading vipers were another story. The viper isn't poisonous either, but it believes the best defense is a good offense, and it mimics the cobra's attack posture. Now I knew there were no cobras in Kentucky, but a viper could spread his neck and sway back and forth in a most convincing manner. My fears overcame my reason, and more than once I chopped a viper into small pieces with my hoe.

"Son, a viper's not poisonous," my father would say. "Snakes kill mice. They're a farmer's friend." I believed him and I didn't believe McBee's folklore, but I'd always slip one piece of the snake into my pocket and feed it to the hogs later to keep that viper from pulling itself together and crawling off after sundown.

The blacksnake in the maple tree was different. The blacksnake was big, well over seven feet long. The maple tree was big, four limbs spreading out from a six-foot diameter trunk, shading the whole back of the house. The big limb that ran out toward the brooder house held my swing suspended from a twenty-five foot rope. I liked to climb out on that limb holding on to the branches above and stand over the swing staring down thirty feet to the yard. At least I did until the blacksnake arrived.

My mother saw it first. It was sliding over the stump where Daddy had sawed off the maple's fifth branch when it threatened to fall on the sun porch roof. She told my daddy to get rid of that snake.

"I won't have a snake living in that tree. It'll scare away all the songbirds."

"Well, I'll take it across the road, but I won't kill it. Think how many mice a snake that size will eat.

We caught the snake, put him in a laundry hamper, carried him across the road and turned him loose at the back of the farm.

A few days later we did it again. We did it four times before the day I was climbing the limb, holding onto the branches above, when one of the branches suddenly moved. It was the branch I was holding, and it moved down my arm, around my neck, down my chest, and around my waist.

I was thirty feet off the ground with a seven-foot blacksnake wrapped around me. I wanted to jump. I wanted to tear that snake from my body. But with the yard swaying beneath the yawning space below me, I did everything I could to make my body be still. After a few minutes the snake worked its way down my right leg and went twisting on down the swing rope to the ground.

I felt the same way I did when I wound my swing rope up tight and let it spin me around and around and around. My face felt flushed. The sky wheeled above me.

I lay down on the big limb and hugged it tight until I stopped shaking before I slid down the trunk and went into the house. I was in trouble again with my mother.

"How many times have I told you to give yourself enough time to get to the bathroom? Now go wash up and put on some clean clothes."

"Yes, Ma'am."

I changed my clothes, and we caught the snake again and took him across the road. That time he never made it back. A few days later, I went down to the box to get the mail and there was that snake stretched out flat on the road like one of those lines of tar they patch a crack with. Since he wasn't a Hognose, I knew he wasn't playing dead.

Why I Don't Like Chicken

It was summer and we weren't milking any cows at the time, so it should have been simple.

"Son," my father said, "you're going to have to be the man around here for a while."

"Yes, sir."

Daddy and I were standing by the backdoor as Mother backed the car out of the garage.

"You know what has to be done."

"Yes sir. First I slop the pigs and then I feed the chickens and gather the eggs."

"Check the back pasture spring every day to see that it's running clear for the cattle, and change the chickens' water every day. In the summer, animals need water more than they do food."

My father was going into the hospital for a hernia operation and would be there for five days. I would be in charge of the farm.

"I want you to do the chores without being asked, son. Your mother has enough to worry about without having to keep on top of you. Here are the keys."

The keys to all the locks on the farm hung of one huge key ring. The barn, the smokehouse, the corncrib, the brooder house, the tool shed, the garage, the hen house, and the meat house. I would not need most of them since it was summer. The cattle were turned out to pasture. We would not use the smokehouse till after the first hard freeze, when we would get together with McBee and some other neighbors and kill the pigs. The garage door was open since Mother had the car out. There was enough corn stored in the hen house for a week or two. All I had to do was shell it and crack it for the chickens. I would need the hen house key, and I would need the meat house key.

"I think we'll just nibble on ham while your daddy's in the hospital," my mother said from the driver's seat. "What do you think, son?"

"That would be fine with me."

"Ham and eggs and grits and gravy for breakfast?"

"Yes'm, sounds fine."

"Good. You bring one in while I'm taking your daddy to the hospital."

My father handed me the big ring of keys, got in the car, and was driven off to the Booth Memorial Hospital in Covington, ten miles north of our farm at White's Tower, Kentucky.

He was right to say that about my doing the chores without being asked. I was at an age when I was just as likely to think I was boarding a ship with Captain Blood or breaking into the Bastille with the Scarlet Pimpernel as I was to think I was walking through the backyard to get the eggs. I could watch the shapes of clouds and see the battle of the Spanish Armada in the wind-tossed apple trees of our orchard during thunderstorms.

Often it took a strong sound from the present to bring me back, like the sound of my father's voice—or the click of a lock.

This time it was the click of a lock, the huge padlock on the meat house door. The sugar-cured ham wrapped in brown paper inside a Bracken Belle Flour bag was crooked in my right arm as I snapped the padlock on the meat house and realized that the keys were still inside. The click sounded like the cell door closing on Sidney Carton.

The meat house was, in fact, very much like the Bastille. Impregnable. It was set on a thick fieldstone foundation that went deep into the ground because, although we hung meat in it, the house was actually a springhouse and a cooling shed for milk. Inside, down three stone steps, a two-foot-wide stone trough ran along the back wall. A spring trickled through it and kept the meat house cool even in the hottest, driest weather.

To keep the coolness in (more than to keep anyone out), the meat house was constructed out of 4 x 8's set sideways so that the walls were eight inches thick. The door was massive and fit into the walls so that no hardware other than the hasp strap and staple eye was visible. There were no windows. And while the door kept the coolness in effectively, it just as effectively kept me out.

I thought about getting the bolt cutters out of the garage and cutting the shackle on the lock, but somehow I did not feel that my father would approve of that solution. Instead I faced five days of running the farm with no keys.

The pigs were no problem. I slopped them with the leftovers from the kitchen, threw some corn in their trough, and ran a little water into their mud wallow with a hose. I thought pigs were wonderful. They could turn field corn (which no one could eat) and turnips (for which I had no use at all) into bacon, which is about the best thing you can put in your mouth.

Chickens were another thing entirely. A hen house in summer smells like no other place on earth. Dust and straw and feathers and chicken shit and an occasional spoiled egg. I always did the chickens as quickly as I could and breathed as little as possible in the process.

Besides the smell, I had to deal with the downright orneriness of the chickens. The hens would often stay on their eggs in the nest, and I had to shoo them before I gathered the eggs. Some of the more ornery hens would not shoo, and I had to endure them pecking on my arms as I reached under their hot, heavy bodies for the eggs.

With the keys locked in the meat house, the only way I could get into the hen house was through the chicken run at the back of the house. I had to place a five-gallon bucket of water in the run door, then crawl up the chicken walk and squeeze through the small door, pushing the bucket of water ahead of me.

This process placed me directly under the wire mesh chicken roost, where the hens spent the night and set me up for a six-foot crawl through a year-old, two-inch-thick patina of chicken shit. The smell was awful but the feel was worse; the chicken shit squished up between my fingers and reminded me of the day we cleaned out the cistern.

There were three sources of water on the farm: a well, a rain barrel, and a cistern. The well was a thirty-five-foot-deep, rock-lined shaft that contained the coolest, sweetest water I ever tasted. We used the well water for bathing, drinking, and cooking. The rain barrel was a cedar cask that caught water off the garage roof. This water was clean and sweet smelling and so soft that we brought it in by the bucketful and used it to rinse our hair. The cistern was on the other side of the house and caught the rainwater off the roof. The cistern water was dank, viscous, and foul smelling. We used it to flush the toilets and wash the car and water the livestock and the lawn.

Sometimes in dry weather the well gave out and we had to switch the pipes and use cistern water.

It was terrible.

Finally it occurred to my father that since the good water in the rain barrel was run-off just like the bad water in the cistern, there must be something wrong with the cistern. He decided to clean the cistern.

He rented a pump from the farmer's co-op in Independence, Kentucky, and pumped all the murky black water out of the cistern into the storm ditch by the highway. When that was done, he discovered that he was too big to get through the hole in the cistern cap.

"Son, looks like you'll have to go down and clean it out." My father laughed as he patted his stomach, which hung over his belt buckle like a down pillow. "I've been sitting too close to the table too long to get through that hole."

We rigged a light so I could see, and I stood with one foot in a bucket while my father winched me down into the murky hole with a block and tackle he'd rigged over the cistern. I don't know if I was glad for the light or not. In the dark I would not have been able to see the viscous mass of rotten vegetation and who knows what else that clogged the bottom of the cistern. I would only have been able to feel the slime and smell the overpowering stench.

Bucket by bucket, I sent the fetid mulch up to my father, who dumped it into fifty-gallon drums set in the back of the pick-up. After the last of the muck was out, my father sent down the garden hose, and I sprayed the cistern with fresh well water that we pumped out after I came up in the bucket.

I was so filthy when I came out of the cistern that I nearly ran the well dry showering, and my mother had my father bury the jeans I had worn. She said no amount of washing could remove the stench.

When the cistern filled up again, it was clean and clear but not as sweet or as cool as the well.

It had taken me most of one afternoon standing up in hip boots to clean the cistern, but now I was faced with five days, morning and night, of crawling through fresh manure.

Crawling through that smelly slime was bad enough, but the hens on the wire mesh roost added to the collection on the floor whenever the spirit moved them. The spirit seemed to move them more when they were excited. And the form of their potential benefactor crawling beneath them definitely excited them. They literally shit on the hands that were about to feed them—the hands, the arms, the back, the legs. I wore a cap and a long sleeved shirt and jeans, so most of this did not bother me beyond the notion of it. However, there was one black and white speckled hen with one eye gone from some former meanness that delighted in sitting on the edge of the roost and shitting with the accuracy of veteran bombardier right on the back of my neck.

The first day I thought, "Beginner's luck." But she did it again the next time and the next and the next. She never had a slump. I tried to trick her by darting my head out quick and pulling it back, but she held her load and waited till I was exposed and then let me have it.

I know dogs can sense when you are afraid of them. My father always said you have to stand up to a dog and let it know who's boss. I remember that's what Ivan Veteshevesky did when he kicked Tuck's dog through the hedge fence. He let that little three-legged fice terror know who was boss. I was never good at letting dogs know who was boss. If I had to walk past a big mean dog on the way home from school, I tried to figure another way to walk home. I was no better with chickens, but there was no other way I could get into the hen house. And my father was depending on me to take care of the farm.

Each day when I went in to shell and crack the corn, I had to tear a little piece of paper off the bag of crushed oyster shells we put out for grit for the chicken craws and use it to wipe the chicken shit off my neck. I really hated the way the paper slid across my neck. It sent a chill down my back, and it was no use trying to tell myself it was something else.

When my daddy came home from the hospital, he said I'd done a good job taking care of things. When I told him about the keys, he said, "Go to the garage and get the bolt cutters and cut that lock off of there. We'll get a new one at the co-op. What do you think bolt cutters are for?"

I cut the lock off the meat house door and retrieved the keys. Then my mother said, "Son, since your father is home, I'm going to fry us up a chicken tonight. Would you go down to the hen house and get me one?"

Prayers are answered. I flew across the yard and opened the lock and scouted around the hen house for my black and white speckled nemesis. She was sitting on the edge of the roost, lined up with the chicken run door, waiting for me. I took her by surprise, swept her from the roost by both legs, and carried her, squawking and squirming and pecking my hand, toward the back porch, where my father was waiting by the chopping block.

"Son, that's a Plymouth Rock. That's one of our better hens. You should have brought one of the leghorns."

"You want me to go back?"

"No. We have God's plenty of chickens. One more or less won't make any difference. Give it here."

"No, sir. I'd like to do this one."

"Well, I never thought I'd live to see this. You know how to use the hatchet?" he asked, offering it to me.

"I won't need it," I said, reaching down and grabbing the hen by its head. I cocked my arm, then snapped the hen like a buggy whip, the way I'd seen my uncle Eddie do it countless times. It worked. I stood there with the hen's one-eyed head in my hand while the headless body raced across the yard, thumped down and began that stupid blood-spurting dance.

After the hen bled out, I scalded it, plucked its feathers, and took it in to my mother, who gutted it, cut it up, and fried it.

She served it with mashed potatoes and gravy and green beans. My father said it was better than any of the food they gave him in the hospital. I don't know. I didn't eat any. The smell of the frying chicken got all mixed up in my mind with the smell of the hen house. I couldn't eat it. I had a bologna sandwich, and I never ate fried chicken again.

Walter Savage and his Low Moan

We were headed up the twisting, nine-mile logger's road from town to Bear Lake to go trout fishing. Uncle Bill was driving Corky, the old Model A Ford. Daddy was in the front with Bill. I was in the back with Walter Savage and the fishing tackle box.

"Walter, Bill was telling me about the last time the two of you were up here," Daddy said with a little laugh.

"Your brother-in-law's crazy. Did you know that? Just plain nuts," said Walter.

"Now, Walter," said Uncle Bill as he touched the horn and then eased the Ford around a right-hand, hairpin turn.

"'Now Walter,' nothing! You could have killed us both. Hit that horn again. The next curve is a real bad one."

"Well, Walter, I didn't, did I?" said Bill. "And we're the only two men on earth who ever free-wheeled from Bear Lake into town and lived to tell about it."

"I'll tell you what. This road's bad enough when you ride the brakes all the way. If I'd knowed what you had in mind that day, right now I'd be the only man to have ever walked it with a string of trout."

Bill blew the horn again and wound the Ford around another switchback turn.

"You should have seen him," Bill said to Daddy. "He was sittin' right there where you are. Wouldn't even look. There we were, coasting into history, and all he did was put his head down and moan the whole way down."

"Is that right, Walter?" asked Daddy.

"Sure is. I was scared. I'm still scared with him driving. I tell you what. I wouldn't be here today if Lefevers hadn't brought in that stringer full of browns yesterday.... My Lord! Look out!"

By the time Walter shouted, I was nearly asleep on the back seat, so it was a real surprise when I got tossed on the floor as Uncle Bill ran the right front wheel up the embankment. I crawled back onto the seat next to the fishing tackle box and looked out the windshield between Daddy's head and Uncle Bill's. All I could see was a huge truck radiator and the rain.

"Well, we damn near bought it that time," whispered Walter.

Uncle Bill, Walter, and Daddy got out and met two men from the truck in the road. I got out and took a good look at the truck. It was a flatbed Mack, loaded with hardwood, headed for the sawmill at the foot of the mountain. It had stopped with its right front wheel on the edge of a cut which dropped away about two hundred feet.

"Y'all were driving that truck too fast for this road," said Uncle Bill.

"Didn't nobody ever learn you that you was supposed to horn your way 'round these narry roads?"

"We did blow, but you were running that truck so hard that you just didn't hear us," said Walter.

The two loggers started to close in on us, and Daddy said, "What are we going to do now? There's no place to turn around, and we can't go by."

"You're gonna back down the mountain," said the fat logger.

"Like hell, I am," said Uncle Bill.

"Course, if you don't wanta back that junk outen the way, we can always pitch it offen the clift."

"Come on, boys. There's three of us and only two of them," said Uncle Bill as he took a step closer to the taller logger.

It was then that I saw the third man. He came walking down the embankment as casually as a banker walking down Main Street. He was a good six feet eight, and he was carrying a muzzle-loader. He hip-leveled the rifle on us, looked over the car and stared at the license. Then he spit off the cliff and said, "Kintucky," as if it were a bad word. "Hell, I could whup a sackful of Kintuckians before breakfast." Then he looked down at me. "Gawd, but they do grow 'em puny, don't they? Boy, you better put you a fistful of them road rocks in your pocket 'fore you blow offen that clift."

Looking at the rifle must have made Uncle Bill forget whatever it was he had in mind. We all scrambled back into the car. Daddy hung out one side and I hung out the other giving directions to Uncle Bill while he tried to keep that old Ford going fast enough so the Mack didn't run up on the hood. Walter Savage had been there before. He was no help at all. He just put his head down on the fishing tackle box and moaned, sort of low, all the way down.

Chicken Gizzards

Daddy and his daddy, Pap, and Daddy's brother-in-law, Uncle Eddie, all loved to eat. Whenever our family got together, it was around a table, a table loaded with food. I always hoped for ham, but their favorite was fried chicken, and there was usually a heaping platter of fried chicken flanked by steaming bowls of green beans and mashed potatoes and gravy.

Besides liking chicken, they all three liked the gizzard best of all, and down underneath all those wings and drumsticks and thighs and whatnot was the one gizzard.

I think it all started one Sunday when Pap picked up the platter, smiled sheepishly, and said, "Would any of y'all like this here chicken craw?" "Don't mind if I do," said Daddy, and he forked the gizzard right off the platter. Pap's eyes went hard. He just sat there holding that empty platter with both hands. Finally he set it down and said, "I see." From then on we all understood that it was war, and it lasted for years.

At first it was rather crude. Daddy took a wing and passed the chicken to Uncle Eddie. He slid the back off the platter and casually swept the gizzard with it. I could tell by the way they looked at him when he set the empty platter down that he had broken the rules and that the last easy victory had been won.

Piece by piece another Sunday's chicken was eaten, and the three of them finally sat there staring at the gizzard. When Pap's wife, Lucy, asked, "One of you going to eat that thing?" she was ignored. Finally Pap made his move. There was an awful din of clashing metal and screaming. Pap forked the gizzard. Daddy, like an old-time sheriff letting the hired gun slap leather first, nailed that gizzard to the platter with his fork, and Uncle Eddie, who, being right-handed was at a disadvantage having to reach across, stuck his fork in the back of Pap's hand.

It was about then that strategy was introduced. "My Gawd. It looks like Fronk's barn's on fire," yelled Pap. Daddy and Uncle Eddie didn't see any fire out the window. When they turned back, they didn't see any gizzard either, and Pap was laughing so hard he nearly choked on it. After that there were so many visions that you would have thought we were a family of Roman Catholics instead of dyed-in-the-wool, dull-as-paint Presbyterians. Pap saw things out the window. Daddy saw things out the backdoor. Uncle Eddie, who sat facing the china cupboard, was again at somewhat of a disadvantage. One time he told about the woman selling Bibles door-to-door, whose panties fell off right in the middle of her sales spiel, and gobbled the gizzard whole while Pap and Daddy were laughing. Another time he just sat staring up at the ceiling. That didn't work. Pap said, "You can't treat us like a bunch of greenhorns at the county fair. That ceiling's been up there since the house was built, and I ain't taking my eyes off that gizzard."

Toward the end nobody believed anybody or anything. One Sunday afternoon the fire bell rang, and the three of them just sat there staring at the gizzard, each of them convinced that one of the other two had paid Curley Beckett to ring the bell.

It all came to an end on Thanksgiving. They hunted all morning and came in to a big chicken dinner. When all the wings and legs and whatnot were gone, there on the platter were three gizzards. "Mr. Macklin gave them to me extra when I bought the chicken," said Lucy. "Now we really have something to be thankful for." They ignored her. They just sat there sullenly looking at those three gizzards. Pap finally forked one of them and groused, "Who the hell ever heard of a chicken havin' three gizzards?"

The Discovery of Electricity

Baseball meant the Cincinnati Reds and Waite Hoyt on the radio. In the summer, whenever Billy and Bobby and I weren't in the woods mimicking our favorite players, I was at home listening to Waite Hoyt give his heart-stopping, eyewitness account from the press box high above Crosley Field—or, if the Reds were on the road, recreate the game in the studio from a skimpy wire report from the site.

Waite Hoyt was best when there was a rain delay. The ex-Yankee pitcher and Hall-of-Famer from the days of Ruth and Gehrig could tell endless interesting tales, not only about his legendary Yankee teammates but about baseball players in general—Shoeless Joe Jackson, Honus Wagner, Grover Cleveland Alexander, Homerun Baker. He had stories about all of them, and I loved to hear them.

I listened to Waite Hoyt on an Atwater Kent console-radio, that stood next to the davenport in our living room. It was there that I sat on Sunday afternoons and listened to the *Lux Radio Theater*, the *Fat Man*, the *Shadow*, and the *FBI in Peace and War*.

As a general rule no one but my father tuned the radio, and it was always unplugged after each use for fear that lightning would strike nearby and burn it up. Our toaster was always unplugged for the same reason.

It was a Sunday. The Reds were in St. Louis for a four-game series with the Cards. They won on Friday night, lost Saturday, and were playing a double-header beginning at noon Central and

1:00 PM Eastern Time. Saturday's game was great because of a fight in the sixth inning that cleared the benches and led to the ejection of a half dozen players on each team. I couldn't wait to see if the hostility carried over to Sunday's games.

I was waiting for my father to get home from church to turn on the radio. It was rough, because my father liked to shake hands with everyone and be the last person out of the church door, even when Waite Hoyt was about to take the air for the Burger Brewing Company.

I went into the kitchen and asked my mother if I could turn the radio on.

"You know your father doesn't like anyone else to tune it."

"It's already on the right station. We listened to last night's game. Please, Mom, can I?"

"Well, all right. Just plug it in and turn it on. If it's not right, you'll have to wait for your father."

My sprint from the kitchen, through the dining room, to the living room may have been the beginning of my track career. I squatted down in front of the radio, felt around for the wire, and jammed it into the floor socket.

What happened next, I wouldn't fully understand until I watched Doc Klein hook a frog's leg up to a dry cell battery in high school biology.

The wire I grabbed was the cotton-covered, copper aerial for the radio. When I rammed it into the floor socket, I proved that both copper and cotton conduct electricity very efficiently. Since I was squatting on my heels, my legs were doubled up pretty much like the frog's. That jolt straightened them out in a flash, and I went flying backwards across the living room and struck the back of my head on Mother's rocking chair.

When I came to, my head hurt and the room smelled of ozone. I screamed, and my mother came running from the kitchen. She calmed my crying; then she plugged the radio in.

It was raining in St. Louis, and Waite Hoyt was siting in a studio in Cincinnati telling stories about Hack, Herman, and Galan.

They were wonderful stories. Eventually my dad came home, and we ate baked ham, sweet potatoes, and butterbeans. The rain stopped in St. Louis, and Waite Hoyt wove his magic with the telegraph wire. We listened as the Reds lost two more to the Cards.

After the game, my dad tried to explain to me about electricity.

"And so you see, son, that caused your muscles to contract and sent you across the room. You hit the rocking chair with the back of your head. That was what caused that bump."

I had to admit it sounded right. But I had been there for the blue flash and the crack and the pain. They were instantaneous, and nothing my father said convinced me that the electricity had not put that lump on my head.

Escape

I was the luckiest kid I knew. None of my friends had older brothers who would play with them, the way mine did.

My brother was a high school senior in 1945. He didn't have to worry about getting out and looking for a job. When he graduated, he shook hands with the principal, walked across the stage, and was inducted into the army.

He knew it was coming. During his senior year he took an army cartography course that involved a light table, tracing paper, and pencils in more colors that I had ever seen before.

I loved to draw. My father brought reams of paper home from work for me, and I had a box of Crayola crayons in my room with sixty-four colors, including my favorite, cinnamon brown. But my brother was drawing maps. Maps were adventures. Pirates had maps to show where the treasure was. I wanted to help make maps.

When I was younger, I always wanted to help my brother. He had a paper route when I was about three. One day I was playing in a tub of water in the backyard, and I took off my swimming suit and followed him around his route, redistributing papers. He tossed one into someone's yard; I came along behind him and tossed it somewhere else. When I got home the phone was ringing off the wall with complaints about missing papers and reports of a little naked paperboy. My brother was never very pleased with my help, but I loved to help him.

"You need any help?"

"I'm doing my homework."

"I want to make maps too."

"You get your crayons and some paper, and you can sit at my desk and make maps."

I did, but my maps looked stupid. I wanted to make real maps with the compass and the triangles and the T-square and all those beautiful light colors.

"Can I help you make your map?"

"No. I have to turn this in tomorrow for a grade."

"I can help good."

"No."

Now most brothers at this point would have tossed me out on my ear and locked the door. A kid down the street had an older brother so mean that he used to say, "I won't let you be my brother unless you give me a penny." The kid fell for it every time. If he had a penny, he would turn it over on the spot. If not, he would spend the day wandering around the neighborhood looking for a pop bottle to take to the store for the deposit. What a dumb kid.

Instead of throwing me out, my brother played games with me. First we played hide-and-seek.

"I know what. We'll play hide-and-seek. You go hide, and after a bit, I'll come and find you.

"Neat."

Hide-and-seek didn't work out too well. I hid in the wicker clothes hamper on the upper landing of the stairs. I waited very quietly for a long, long time. Finally I decided my hiding place was too good for my brother to discover. I decided to give some clues. First, I made a little sniffing sound. Then I coughed quietly. Finally I began to rock the wicker hamper back and forth.

Since the hamper was nearly full of clothes, and I made it top heavy, my third clue sent me and the hamper banging down the nine steps to the bottom landing. I was OK—a little nicked up and scared to death—but OK. The hamper was in bad shape. It had split open and spilled me and the pile of dirty clothes down the steps, then followed me down, rolling over me on the landing and crashing against the wall. It would never be the same.

My mother came running from the kitchen where she was fixing supper, and my father put down *The Kentucky Times-Star* and came striding in from the living room.

"My stars! What on earth is going on?"

"What are you doing, son?

"We're playing hide-and-seek."

By this time my brother was at the top of the stairs.

"Oh, there you are. You really had me fooled. I had no idea where you were."

"My hamper. Look what you've done to my hamper."

"Son, your brother is busy with his homework. I don't want you bothering him. You go to your room and find something to do until supper. I'll see if I can fix your mother's hamper."

My father worked on the hamper, and we continued to use it. But after its trip down the stairs, it looked like the leaning tower of laundry.

That was the last time we played hide-and-seek. My brother came up with a new game, escape.

"Hi, what'cha doin'?"

"Homework."

"Can I help?"

"No. But we can play escape if you want."

Escape was neat. My brother would tie me up with Mother's old clothesline and toss me up on the third shelf in the linen closet on top of the quilts, and then I would try to escape. Sometimes I was a prisoner of the Apaches; sometimes I was Harry Houdini.

Now and then I escaped before dinner, and we had time to play again. Usually my brother trussed me up in a fashion that would make a midshipman green with envy. My brother knew his knots—and I would still be playing when Mother called us to supper. My brother would roll me out of the closet, untie me, and send me off to wash my hands.

"You young men were so quiet up there. What were you doing?' my mother asked.

"I was working on my maps."

"And what were you doing, James?"

"I was playing escape. I was a prisoner of the Nazis. I was tied up in the closet, and I had to escape to tell the Allies about the German battle plans."

"Tied up in the closet," said my mother. "Such an imagination."

It was neat. None of my friends had older brothers or sisters who would play with them, and my brother played escape with me nearly every night.

Tippy's Headache

My brother had a dog named Tippy. Tippy was stupid. He was stupid in the normal ways that dogs can be stupid. He chewed up shoes and furniture and rugs. He dug holes in the flowerbeds. He barked at anyone who walked past the house, and he delighted in intimidating the postman.

Tippy was also stupid in special ways. He chased airplanes. Actually, he chased the shadows of airplanes.

When I was young, airplanes were subsonic propeller-driven jobs. When you heard a plane and looked up, you saw a plane. Now when you hear a plane, you look up and see the contrail where the plane used to be.

Tippy never looked up when he heard a plane. He looked down and chased the shadow across the yard. To be fair to Tippy, he also chased the shadows of butterflies. Butterflies floated about the yard, checking out the flowers, and Tippy yipped and bounded eccentrically after them. The airplanes moved with much more directness than the butterflies. Their shadows, while they might crawl and slither up over the sandbox or the swing, moved in a straight line across the yard from fence to fence. The airplane shadows, being insubstantial, moved with ease through the fence. Tippy, being more substantial than many things, encountered considerable difficulty in his attempts to follow the planes' shadows through the fence.

He would hit the worn fence at full speed, bounce off, roll over, shake himself, and then get on with his life. He never remembered or learned much from these encounters because he would yip and challenge the shadow of the very next plane that dared to glide over our yard.

Since chasing airplane shadows was essentially a self-destructive habit, everyone was amused by it. Tippy's other habit did not amuse us as much. He liked to piss on the floor registers. Actually he didn't do it often enough to call it a habit, but he did it often enough for us to be ever vigilant.

Tippy was not allowed in the house. The moment he got in, he headed for a register. The moment he got near the heat rising from the register, he cocked a leg and cut loose. It happened only once or twice, but the smell lingered the way the odor of boiled cabbage does. We remembered it. And we saw to it that Tippy stayed in the yard.

Then one cold winter day, the front door bell rang. My mother dried her hands and walked from the kitchen across the dining room and living room to the door. She opened it, and there stood the preacher, the Reverend Brown.

"Well, Reverend Brown."

"Good afternoon, Mrs. Perkins. I was down at the hospital and I thought I'd drop in to see you while I was in the. . ."

The Reverend Brown never got the word "neighborhood" out of his mouth. Just at that moment, Tippy raced across the snow-covered porch, through the minister's legs, and past my mother, heading straight for the floor register in the dining room.

Mother spun from the door and followed Tippy on a dead run, leaving the Reverend Brown alone and confused in the blowing snow of the front porch.

"Tippy. You stay away from that register, you hear? You'll...you'll get a headache."

Now, most people wouldn't understand the relationship between heat and a dog's headache, but we understood Mother's elliptical warning.

If Tippy pissed on the floor register with the minister in the house, my mother would be embarrassed and she would clobber the dog with whatever heavy object presented itself. That action would lead to a headache.

Tippy was stupid, but he wasn't dumb. He understood Mother's statement clearly, and he darted from the register to the cover of the dining room table as she closed the distance between them.

"Don't just stand there," she shouted to the minister. "Help me head him off. Heat makes him sick. He gets terrible headaches. We have to get him outside."

"Oh," said the Reverend Brown as he bent over to pull his rubbers off before coming into the house.

By the time the Reverend Brown had shucked his overshoes, Mother had grabbed a broom from the kitchen and was whaling away under the dining room table, trying to do serious damage to Tippy.

Tippy liked a good game as well as anyone, so he clamped down on the broom straw with his teeth, growled, and began pulling Mother under the table. Mother was having none of it. She shifted her weight, pivoted, and swung the broom, dog and all, out from under the table and straight through the glass front of the china cupboard. The impact was tremendous. There was glass everywhere, the shelves collapsed, and not a single piece of Grandmother's Limoges service for twelve survived.

Then it all really broke loose. Tippy scrambled out of the shattered cupboard and headed back for the cover of the table as Mother threw the shards and debris of her Sunday china at his retreating form.

With broken cups and saucers and dinner plates crashing all about him, the Reverend Brown said, "Oh my," and removed himself to the relative safety of the still-open front door.

As Mother's rage subsided, her targeting abilities increased, and it was soon clear to Tippy that the dining room table provided no real protection from ricocheting Limoges. As she paused to re-arm herself with a piece of a salad plate, he headed for the front door.

The Reverend Brown moved into the living room, stepping carefully to avoid the shattered china. Mother shut the door and asked, "Would you like some tea?"

"Some tea would be very nice."

"Well, you just sit down here, and I won't be a minute."

The Reverend Brown sat down on one of the several uncomfortable rose velvet Victorian chairs in the living room. He was trying to sort things out. He remembered knocking on the door. He remembered my mother opening the door. He remembered the dog. After that things got confusing.

My mother returned with the tea for the Reverend Brown in one of her serviceable everyday cups. He balanced his tea and conversed casually with my mother, who sat opposite him on the couch and talked calmly about the number of women needed to serve the mission dinner, as if that room and the next were not strewn with the debris of her best china, which she had, moments ago, hurled at a dog because the dog might get a headache. The Reverend Brown, who was having some difficulty caring about the upcoming mission dinner, went over the events concerning the dog again and again, trying to see what had actually occurred. After several attempts, he gave up, deciding that he had been chasing shadows.

Butterbeans

1.

My little cars were made of wood with thread spools cut in half for wheels. My father made them at his workbench in the basement. While he worked, I watched and played with wood chips and planing curls. Sometimes I was allowed to make a lath sword and sally forth up the cellar steps into the backyard to the quarterdeck of my Spanish galleon. Sometimes I was allowed to shape a boat to play with during bath time. And sometimes I was allowed to play with the wonderful red pot-metal Model A Ford that belonged to my brother before the war.

"Why can't I have one like this one?" I said, running the red car down the length of the workbench toward my father.

"They need all the metal for the war," my father said.

I knew about that need. I went around the block with my wagon collecting scrap metal for the war.

When my brother was in high school, he was in a contest to see who could collect the most scrap metal. He collected a lot, but he didn't win. A girl won who donated a cast iron railroad bridge from an abandoned right of way on her father's farm.

They needed a lot of things for the war. They needed my brother. He was in the army somewhere.

They needed my father. After days at school, where he was a principal, he worked nights in a factory that made bomb fuses.

They needed my uncle. He made huge wooden gliders in the Baldwin Piano plant in Cincinnati and whittled intricate folk art in his spare time.

They needed shoes for all the soldiers so shoes were rationed.

I got new shoes more often than Mother or Father because my feet were growing so fast.

"I don't know what we're going to do with this boy," my mother said. "He's growing so fast we can't keep him in shoes."

"Put a brick on his head," a helpful neighbor suggested.

"Take him to the shoe exchange," said another.

"Yeh, Louie might have a pair that would fit him."

2.

Louie Martz ran a shoe repair business on Twentieth Street between Garrad and Greenup and took out-grown shoes in payment for repairs. These he fixed up and offered to his regular customers for either cash or trade. It was a little black market operation that avoided the need for ration stamps. There were never enough stamps to keep growing boys in shoes anyway, and after I ate the ration book, we didn't have stamps for a year so it was a good thing Louie was around. He kept me in shoes during the war.

I loved to go to Louie's shop. It was the dirtiest place I'd ever been, and Louie was the dirtiest man I'd ever seen. The shop was small and crammed full of shoe-making machinery: sewing machines, lasts, shapers, and buffers. Louie did more than repair shoes. If you could afford it, he would trace your feet on butcher paper and make you a pair of one-of-a-kind-shoes.

Louie always wore a long-sleeved blue cotton work shirt with the sleeves rolled up to his elbows and heavy denim bib overalls. Whenever I went into his shop, his clothes and arms and face were covered with a patina of machine oil, shoe leather dust, and soot from the coal stove that dominated the small area in front of the counter where customers sat in three unpainted, wooden kitchen chairs. The shop was hot, summer and winter. In the summer the sun boiled through the soot-covered window and was stored in the black fastness of the small shop. In the winter the coal stove, which was large enough to do justice to a small house, turned the 12 x 12 shop into near liquid.

As a result of this heat and his bulk, Louie was always sweating, and the sweat cut gullies in the grime on his face and hands. The heat also increased the customer's awareness of aromas. Added to the dirt, shoe leather, and engine oil smells, there was the odor of Louie's favorite lunch: onion, black bread, and beer.

What fascinated me most about Louie was his mouth. Louie chewed tobacco with one side of his mouth, held a mess of shoe nails between his lips on the other side, and spoke broken English with a heavy German accent out of the middle.

"Ich kam here in 1935. Hitler was not gud for Chermany. I leave."

Louie and my father talked about Hitler a lot. Louie would swear, "Mine Gott, Hitler. He is being a madman." Sometimes for emphasis he would spit out of the chew side of his mouth across the counter and hit the stove with a sizzle, all without dropping a single nail out of the other side.

Other times, Louie would make me laugh. "Dis boy have grow a voot since last time. Is gud. Now I zell to him tree chuse."

On Saturday, when everyone was off work and families walked around the neighborhood visiting and shopping, Louie's shop was always closed.

"Louie is a Jew, son," my father said. "He's lucky he left Germany when he did."

"Why?" I asked.

"Let's stop at the dairy and get an ice cream," my father said. "What flavor would you like?"

"Strawberry."

3.

I didn't know where Billy and Bobby were. I walked over to their houses and called, but they were gone. I had to play with Nancy. She always wanted to play house, but I said that we were going to play little cars or I was not going to play at all.

So I was playing little cars with Nancy in the soft brown dirt in the cool between the two dirty red-brick, three-storied houses at 2115 and 2117 Maryland Avenue. Mrs. Molique was sitting in the sun on the wooden back fence that divided my yard from Nancy's. She had her feet stretched out to her back steps. She was shelling butterbeans into a yellow bowl held between her knees and dropping the hulls into her apron in her lap.

The backyard was just like it always was—the big wooden swing, the sandbox where Daddy found the black widow spiders, the two big maple trees, and the red and purple hollyhocks that fuzzed us sticky when we hid in them.

And then while I was playing little cars, right there with Nancy, Mrs. Molique screamed and threw butterbeans all over my backyard. Now the backyard was different. And I was afraid. I ran into the house, and there stood Mother by the stove waving a large black cast-iron skillet.

"Why did Nancy's mommy fall off the fence?"

"The war is over! The war is over! The war is over!" My mother grabbed me and hugged me, saying the same thing over and over again.

I ran out and told Nancy, and she said she hoped the war would be over tomorrow too because her mommy was so happy. Then church bells started ringing, sirens screamed, horns honked, and we played little cars.

4.

When Mrs. Molique fell off the fence, she broke her arm, but the cast was off by the time her husband came back from the

South Pacific. Now Nancy had a father, too. Our families cooked out in the backyard at night, and we played hide-and-seek with the big maple tree as home.

"Things are returning to normal," my mother said.

Nothing seemed normal to me. Everything was changing. Everything was new and different and exciting. We got new tires for the car and took drives on Sunday out into the country to look for farmland. We bought meat at Schulte and Wisher's without ration stamps and went shopping for new shoes in Cincinnati.

To get to Cincinnati my mother and I rode the trolley car that stopped on the car tracks at the end of Maryland Avenue. It went from there down Garrad Street to Twentieth, up Twentieth to Greenup and down Greenup to Court Street, where it jogged over a half block to line up with the suspension bridge.

When the bridge was begun in 1856 by John Roebling, the man who later designed the Brooklyn Bridge, the ferry boat operators were a strong enough lobby to see to it that the bridge didn't meet any streets in either Covington or Cincinnati.

On the Cincinnati side of the Ohio River, the suspension bridge led straight to The Dixie Terminal where the streetcars from Kentucky turned around. The Terminal was a huge building with three levels of transit landings and an arcade full of shops and restaurants. After the war, it had something else I'd never seen, disabled veterans, men with no arms, men with no legs, blind men, men swathed in bandages. All of them were selling something; pencils, booklets, flowers, apples, anything they could sell to get by. Some of them wore parts of their uniforms; some of them had signs hung around their necks: "BLIND VET" or "3rd ARMORED."

I walked through the Dixie Terminal Arcade trying to look out the side of my eye at the legless man on a mechanic's crawler. I wanted to look right at him, like I wanted to go to the side show at the Bracken County Fair. My uncle, who used to work for the carnival and told me about geeks, said he would take me to the side show, but my mother said we must never call attention to the infirmities of others.

I walked slowly past the man whose legs ended in leather pads six or seven inches down his thighs. He was wearing an Eisenhower jacket with campaign ribbons on it. He was sitting under a hand-lettered sign that said "LANDMINE/SAIPAN." As I went past him I slowly turned my head and felt my mother's fingers claw a warning into my shoulder.

Near the revolving doors at the Third Street exit of the terminal, a man was selling balloons. They were big and white and floated crazily in the air, blown here and there on their strings by the wind coming through the revolving doors. I had never seen a balloon before. There were no balloons during the war. There was little rubber, and what there was went for tires for military vehicles. I wanted a balloon.

As if to prove my theory that things were not really returning to normal, my mother bought me the balloon.

"Hold on tight. If you let go of the string, it will be gone."

5.

We went to the John Shillitoe Company to look for shoes. The store was crowded and I held on to my mother's skirt with one hand and held tightly to my balloon with the other. When we rode the escalator, I jumped at the bottom to keep from having my toes crushed. I watched my balloon the whole time. It bounced and floated above the heads of the adults who did not seem to see it as the miracle it was.

Finally we settled on some shoes. They fit me fine, but they were brown and boring and designed to move across the earth. I wanted to float. I wanted to rise above the heads of the adults. I wanted to move with the winds. I also wanted to eat.

"I'm hungry."

"Would you like to go to Mills?"

Mills? Mills Cafeteria! I was so excited I almost let go of my balloon. At Mills you could get whatever you wanted. They had everything you could think of, and you could take some of anything.

"Yes'm. I would like that."

"Remember, your eyes are sometimes bigger than your stomach."

That was true. I would wander down the line in Mills and take more than I could ever eat. Mills had a zillion kinds of vegetables, and I loved vegetables. At home I didn't have a choice. I had to eat whatever my mother cooked. No matter how long it took, I had to sit at the table until I ate my dinner. Lima beans and brussels sprouts were no problem, but it was often dark before I managed to swallow the last bite of parsnips. At Mills I could choose. I loved Mills.

We stood in the long line waiting to pick up our silverware and tray. I watched my balloon and tried to guess which vegetables they would have. Finally we got our trays and silver and started to walk down the line of steam tables. I ignored the desserts (I never learned to like sweets) and strained to see the vegetables around the woman in front of me. She could not decide between blackberry cobbler and big slice of lemon meringue pie and did not need either. She finally took the cobbler, and we moved on to the vegetables.

I never did find out what vegetables Mills had lined up to tempt me that day. As soon as my balloon floated over the heated portion of the steam table, it exploded. I screamed in fright and then began crying. My mother could not make me stop. I stood there, holding up the line of customers, with the string, still tight in my hand, tied to a shred of rubber on the floor.

"It's all right, James," she said, trying to dry my tears. "These things happen."

"But I held on tight."

"Sometimes it doesn't matter how tightly you hold on, son. You still lose things."

The Homecoming

I sat in the back seat of the 1937 Packard sedan my father had nursed tenderly through the war. The war was over. I knew that. One warm August afternoon Mrs. Molique, the lady next door, had been sitting on the back fence shelling butterbeans. All at once she screamed and fell off the fence and threw the butterbeans all over my backyard. I had been frightened and had run into the kitchen where my mother had grabbed me and hugged me and said over and over again, "The war is over. The war is over."

Mr. Molique, my playmate Nancy's daddy, wasn't the only one who came back from the war. My Uncle Peck, my father's brother, came back, and we drove to the Union Terminal in Cincinnati to meet his train.

I had to sit back on the seat so I really couldn't see much except the upper floors of buildings and the second stories of houses. I liked to kneel on the seat and look out the window or stand behind the front seat and stare through the windshield, but my mother said that was too dangerous.

There was a fire in one of the buildings on Vine Street, and the police had set up a roadblock to protect the fire hoses. We stopped, and a policeman directed us to a detour to the terminal.

"We'll never be on time now," said my father.

"Sit down, son," said my mother. "How many times have I told you how dangerous it is to stand like that?"

"Yes'm" was all I said. I had no idea how many times she told me that. It was something on the order of the number of times she told me to wash behind my ears or the number of times she told me not to shove my dirty socks under the bed.

Sitting as I had to on the Packard's wide back seat, my feet would not touch the floor, and they went to sleep just as they did every Sunday in church. In church, I sat under a stained glass window, "Jesus, the Shepherd of the lambs," and listened to sermons based on the Golden Rule and the Beatitudes and every week heard a long prayer for peace.

Now there was peace, and as the Packard eased to the curb in front of the train station I wondered what all the soldiers and sailors would do.

"There he is," my mother said. "Over here, Peck," she yelled as she got out of the car waving her arms.

Uncle Peck walked slowly to the car pulling his worn duffel bag behind him. My father got out and opened the backdoor for him.

"Sorry we're late, Peck. There's a big fire down on Vine Street."

"S'alright," said Peck and slid the duffel in beside me.

The Packard was moving again and I could barely see Peck past the huge khaki canvas bag wedged between us. My father took his eyes off the road and turned toward my uncle.

"Well, Peck, how are you?" he asked in his smoothest Kiwanis style and turned his attention back to the road.

"Drunk," Peck mumbled.

"What's that, Peck? I didn't hear you. Nita, did you ever see such traffic in your life?"

"Drunk," Uncle Peck said more loudly this time.

"Oh, my," said my mother.

"Now, Nita," said my father, "don't you be goin' 'oh, my' to Peck. With what he's been through he has a right to get drunk for once. Ain't that right, Peck?"

"Drunk," said Uncle Peck again even more loudly.

In the fall I bought some yellow pencils for school from a man with no legs wearing an Eisenhower jacket full of colorful campaign ribbons. My father studied the ribbons and said the man had served in North Africa with Patton. The man sat on an auto mechanic's creeper in front of Coppin's, the biggest department store in town. Lots of people bought pencils. I was afraid of the man with no legs, as I was of any disabled person.

"Uncle Peck is lucky, isn't he?"

"What?" my father said, counting the change the streetcar conductor handed him.

"Uncle Peck is lucky he didn't get hurt in the war."

"Oh, he got hurt. He nearly got killed. But he's okay now. I'll have him tell you about it sometime."

"Peck," my father said handing my uncle the platter of fried chicken. "I want you to tell the boy about Guadalcanal. I want him to know what you and the other brave young men did for this country of ours."

I watched my uncle's hands reach out toward the platter. They were long, thin, and pale. I hoped that my uncle would leave a drumstick.

Peck took the breast and passed the platter to me. I forked the remaining drumstick and then made a feint toward the gizzard.

"Don't you touch that gizzard, boy," my father snapped. "Me and Peck are going out in the yard and fight over that directly. Ain't that right, Peck?"

Peck didn't say anything.

We ate for a while in silence with my mother slipping in and out of the kitchen to bring in hot rolls and refill tea glasses.

Finally, my father said, "Well, Peck, now that you're full, tell the boy about the war."

Peck didn't say anything. He just sat there looking like he was seeing something far off, and his face got white as his hands. Then he got up and said "excuse me" to my mother and went to the bathroom. I could hear him being sick.

My father and mother and I ate our apple pie in silence. Uncle Peck came out of the bathroom and stood in the open front doorway smoking a cigarette and staring off into the distance.

When I first heard the doorbell begin to ring I was upstairs, and I ran down to answer it, as I always did when it got close to Christmas. I liked to see the size and shape of all packages delivered to my house in December.

I got to the door at the same time as my mother who was drying her hands on her apron. The bell was still ringing. It was still ringing after my mother opened the door. Uncle Peck was leaning against the bell with his head against the doorframe. He was wearing a white shirt and no tie. He was shivering, standing barefoot in the snow on the front porch. Uncle Peck lifted his head and looked at me. "Here, kin," he said. "I brought you a present." I took the paper bag. Inside I found a lead soldier in a combat outfit carrying an M-1 rifle.

My father came into the living room, and my mother shooed me out. "You go upstairs to your room and play for awhile. Grownups have to talk here."

I went to the top step and listened while my father and mother talked to Peck.

"I'm just down on my luck. Seems I can't hold on to nothing since the war."

"You need some clothes. Go upstairs and get him that stuff we set aside for the church. And get those brown shoes, too," my father ordered.

I slipped into my room. As Mother passed in the hall muttering under her breath, she reached in and pulled my door closed. When I heard her go back downstairs, I resumed my post on the top step.

"Well, yes, I'm a little short."

"I can give you $10. I wish it could be more, but we got insurance due this week."

"I thank you so much. You won't be sorry. I'm going to do something with my life. Look for a job. Make something of myself. You'll see. You won't be sorry."

When I heard the door close, I ran into my brother's room and looked out the window onto the snowy street. I watched my Uncle Peck walk down the street, then I heard shouts from the living room.

"He'll drink it up and then he'll sell the coat and then he'll sell the shoes and drink that up, too."

"Nita."

"He will. Mark my word. He will."

"Nita. We owe it to him. He's a hero. Nita. He nearly got himself killed for this country, Nita. He's a hero."

"He's a drunk."

"Nita."

He was buried in his uniform, but it was a closed coffin. Uncle Peck died of carbon monoxide poisoning in the big snow just before Thanksgiving. He was drunk. My father said Uncle Peck was probably afraid to turn up at the home place and face my grandfather. He'd run the car to keep warm. When they found him, the car was out of gas and he'd been dead for two days. My grandfather wouldn't have a thing to do with any of it. The pallbearers were six men from Uncle Peck's old unit. After the funeral, they stood by the fire in our living room and drank and talked to my father.

"Yes, sir. You can say that again, sir. He was a hero."

"If it hadn't been for him, I wouldn't be here. He wiped out a bunch of Japs that had Tony and me pinned down. Right, Tony?"

"Sure, Ralph. Peck was a hero, and now he's with all the rest of them."

I reached up on the mantle and took down the lead soldier Uncle Peck had given me. I dropped it into the fire and watched it melt and run down into a pool on the hearthstone under the grate.

Music Hath Charms

They were brought together as people are who have been a part of something that most people never knew about or, if they ever knew, they have forgotten.

There were two of them, Tuck and the Russian (the dog came along later), and they had been friends (as much as two men who can barely talk to each other can be) since '32 when the Russian had come to try to unionize the Flour Mill where Tuck was the foreman. The Russian failed at that for the same reason that he failed to become close to anyone in his adopted country, failed for the same reason that Communism failed in a country whose economic system had failed—because although he could understand and read English, he had never learned to speak it; because after his few halting attempts to speak to the men at the mill, he settled in to become one of the best workers and confined his speech to "Da" and "Nyet."

At first Tuck had considered Ivan "a Goddamned furiner," but after working with him for twenty years, after learning that he too had been there—("There" was Russia, where Tuck had served in the Allied Expeditionary Force under Brigadier General W. E. Ironside, the British commander in support of the White Army in the Russian Civil War in 1918 and 1919. "There" was Archangel and the Dvina River, which the Allies held with their gunboats. "There" was the vast expanse of Northern Russia, which they tried to hold with too few troops and too long lines of supply against the Reds and against the Russian winter. And "There" was the village of Ust Padenga, the southern defense perimeter for Shenkursk on the Vaga, a tributary of the Dvina where on the nineteenth of January 1919, long after the freezing river had forced their supporting gunboats to withdraw, Tuck's company was surrounded by the Reds in 45 below zero weather. The Americans lost seventeen men. Tuck lost three toes on his right foot to frostbite.)—Tuck's respect for Ivan's hard work and his knowledge that they had both been there, reduced his invective to "that Rooshan."

After a long day at the mill, Tuck would sag into one of the blue kitchen chairs and say to no one in particular (his wife was there stirring the stew for supper, but Tuck hadn't said anything directly to her since the day in April in 1945, just one month before the war ended, when she met him in the front yard with the news that Lonie, their only child, had been killed in Germany): "That Rooshan can carry more flour than any man I ever knew. Someday I'm going to load me a car as fast as that Rooshan."

Tuck's wife would smile and say, "He's twenty years younger than you are. We'll see snow in June before you whip Ivan Veteshevsky loading."

"Then maybe I'll just whip him," Tuck would say again to no one in particular, then add philosophically, "I been doin' man's work all day. You'd think a woman would put something on the table."

Tuck never whipped Ivan loading a car, but they carried on years of nearly one-sided conversations about the Civil War. Never considering Ivan's age, Tuck finally convinced himself that he had once see Ivan in April of 1919 in a gang of Bolshevik prisoners cleaning the streets of Archangel.

"We were there, eh Ivan?"

"Da."

For Ivan, "there" was Ekaterinburg on the sixteenth of July 1918, where as a child of eleven he watched his father and other members of the Ural Territorial Soviet, in the basement of Ipatiev House, shoot the Czar and his family with pistols.

"There" was an abandoned mineshaft thirteen miles from Ekaterinburg where the next day he saw the bodies burned. "There" was also Ekaterinburg leveled and his father hanged by Kolchak. "There" was the hostile steppe where he hid and stole frozen turnips as he worked his way west toward America.

Then there was the dog.

"'Spite the fact he has only three legs, he's the best bird dog in this country." He was too, and Tuck said it so many times, in the years after Mutt had been run clear over by Randall Thompson's Oliver side mower while he was standing on the point by a covey of quail, that folks forgot his name was Mutt and started calling him Spite. It was a good name for Tuck's dog because after Lonie was killed in the war, Tuck quit playing his guitar, and after he was forced to retire from the mill, and Ivan became the foreman, he just sat on his front porch in spite of the world and set Mutt on anyone who walked by the box hedge which divided his yard from the unpaved road beyond.

Colston Renfro's boy, Budda (whose real name was Shabudda and who was named for the little Mississippi town where Samantha Lee, Miz Renfro, was born) had learned from bitter experience to take the corner off Mill Street onto the dirt road in front of Tuck's house at high speed and fling the Brooksville Bugle over the box hedge without slowing down. Sometimes that way the paper landed on the porch roof and sometimes it lit in the honeysuckle in front of the porch, and Tuck called Eliot Whiteside, publisher and editor of the Bugle, more than once to complain about Budda's delivery. But Mr. Whiteside knew Tuck and was never too rough on Buddha, and besides Budda figured it was easier to get chewed out than chewed up.

Of all the people Tuck liked to sic Mutt on, none pleased him more than Ivan Veteshevsky. For Tuck had changed with the country, and by 1953, when the junior senator from Wisconsin was finding a Godless Communist under every bush, Tuck was convinced that the Communists had cost him his job, three toes on his right foot, and his only son. So Tuck loved to bait Ivan as he went back and forth in front of Tuck's house on his way to and from the mill.

"Hey, Rooshan, you still believe we ought to split up all the money?"

"Da."

"Hey, Rooshan, they's a red paint sale on up at Williams'."

"Da."

"Hey, Rooshan, you ever hear from your relations back in Roosha?"

"Nyet."

"Sic 'em, Mutt."

On command the little three-legged fice dog would dart through the gate and circle Ivan Veteshevsky's feet yelping and snapping at his boots. All the players seemed to know their parts. Mutt circled, yelped, and snapped, but he never closed in on Ivan's gigantic legs. Ivan always raised his big fist and shook it at Tuck. Tuck smiled, spat into the honeysuckle, and said, "Get on down the road, Rooshan."

Then one muggy September evening there was a change in the script. Ivan, coming home from a long day on the loading dock at the mill, was met by Tuck's baiting questions, and as he passed the gate, Spite yelped once, sprang, and set his teeth in Ivan's calf.

"Nyet!" Ivan screamed.

"At-a-boy, Mutt. Get 'im," bellowed Tuck as he danced off the steps onto the dying grass of the yard.

"Nyet," screamed Ivan again as he flung his leg out quickly, causing Spite to lose his grip. Ivan panted, bunched his body, screamed "Nyet" once more, and kicked Spite through the box hedge. The yipping, unbalanced bundle rolled right past Tuck, who was frozen in mid-dance by Ivan's unexpected violence.

While Tuck was still standing poised on his left foot, Ivan turned the corner of the hedge and strode toward his home.

"Woman," Tuck roared, "get me my rifle. I'm goin' kill me that Rooshan."

By the time Tuck got the cartridges out of the locked tallboy in the upstairs hall, it was nearly dark on the dirt road. He had never been to Ivan's place. It was farther than he thought. The low clouds darkened the rough road and caused him to lose his footing several times. When he saw the lamplight from Ivan's, he paused, slipped a cartridge into the chamber, then moved slowly forward toward the light. It was then he heard the music—wild yet sad, like two guitars. He stopped. Tuck listened so intently that he was not even aware of the light rain when it began, and when the real storm broke, he turned back toward home and arrived soaked to the skin.

The next day, when Ivan walked by the box hedge on his way to the mill, Tuck was on the front porch softly strumming his guitar.

"Hey, Ivan."

"Da."

"Whatcha call that thing you play?"

"Balalaika."

"Why don't you come up here after work? We'll play a little together."

"Da."

Ivan turned toward the mill, took a few steps, then turned back as Tuck said,

"Hey, Rooshan."

"Da."

"We were there, weren't we?"

"Da."

What's a Friend For?

Wiemann's Delicatessen stood on Eastern Avenue just a block down the Green Line car tracks from my house on Maryland Avenue. Mother didn't like Wiemann's and did her big shopping at the chain stores, but sometimes when the car was gone, she sent me down the tracks for a quart of milk or a box of salt. I liked to go to the store because there was usually change, and change meant candy or a soft drink. Mother knew about little boys and cream soda; she never asked for the change.

Whenever I went to the store, I hid behind the cars along Eastern Avenue and looked Wiemann's over before I went in. I didn't want to run into Dickie Wiemann. He was older, and he wasn't too bright. He liked to beat people up.

On this particular day, I wasn't worried, though. I had Billy North with me. Billy was older too, and Dickie was afraid of Billy. Everybody was afraid of Billy. I walked across the brick street, up the three concrete steps, over the marble entryway, and into the store, like a king, with a quarter in my hand and Billy at my side.

We smelled the heady, pungent smell as we walked barefoot across the grease-sticky wooden floor. Mr. Wiemann was tossing some fresh sawdust around the huge butcher block that looked ominous with the great cleaver stuck into it. Billy stared at the gleaming blade.

"Boy, I bet I could cut your arm off with that," he whispered.

"If I had it, I wouldn't worry about ol' Dickie."

"You don't have to worry about him. I'll take care of him."

"What will it be, boys?"

"I want one stick of butter, Mr. Wiemann."

"One stick of butter. There you are. That will be fifteen cents...out of twenty-five cents. Here's your butter and your dime. Will there be anything else?"

Ol' Wiemann knew I couldn't walk out of that store with 10 cents in my pocket and him with a whole cooler full of cold drinks.

"I'd like a cream soda, please, Mr. Wiemann."

"That'll be ten cents, and you'll have to drink it here."

"Let's drink it outside on the steps."

It was a good idea because the meat smell didn't go so good with cream soda. As he headed for the door, Billy slid his hand along the shelf and snaked a box of animal crackers off it and into his jacket pocket. I felt the pressure of Mrs. Wiemann's eyes as we passed the candy counter near the door. "Stick of butter," I said holding it up, "and one cream soda."

"Is that all?"

"Yes'm," I said, pushing the door open.

The door banged shut behind us, and we were free. I sat down and lifted the bottle of cream soda to my lips. It was then that I saw Dickie leaning against the front of the store.

"Gimme some of your pop."

"No," I said, sliding away from Dickie.

He pulled himself erect and shuffled toward us.

"Gimme some of your pop or I'll hit you one."

Billy ducked into his fighting crouch and snarled, "You hit him and you'll have me to fight. Now get out of here and leave us alone, you queer."

Dickie looked sullenly at Billy for a moment and then pushed past us into the store.

"You sure took care of him."

"Yeh, now give me some pop."

Billy leaned back against the doorframe and turned the bottle up.

"Hey, don't drink it all."

"Why not? I kept you from getting beat, didn't I? So I should get the pop."

"You give me some or I'll tell Ol' Wiemann what you got in your pocket."

Billy stared at me with his eyes blazing. Then he threw the bottle to the pavement and said, "There, drink it."'

When the bottle hit the marble entryway, it exploded, sending a slice of glass into my leg. Blood was everywhere. I looked at the blood, dropped the butter and ran off up the car tracks toward home.

Mother wasn't even mad about the butter, and the next day Billy and I chased an escaped criminal. Billy had winged him in the leg as he went over the prison wall, and it was easy to follow the trail of blood his wound had left on the rocks and the fallen leaves along the car tracks.

71

The Great Train Robbery

The Green Line, which ran ten routes across the Ohio River into Northern Kentucky, was owned by the Covington, Newport and Cincinnati Transit Company when I was growing up. The #8 Eastern Avenue cars made a loop through the woods near my house at the end of Maryland Avenue as they went from Eastern over to Garrad Street for their return trip to Cincinnati. On hot summer afternoons this two-block-long right-of-way, the car tracks, was our haven from the swelter. Bobby Taylor, Billy North, and I would spend hours kicking the piles of leaves that Mr. Johnson dumped in the car tracks to rot, telling each other the biggest lies we could think of, and watching the wonderful trolley cars rumbling down the two blocks of the car tracks.

Usually the modern, green and buff cars with the folding doors and just one driver came rattling up the tracks; however, now and again the traffic would demand an extra car, and one of the wonderful old brown cars from the #5 Holman Street run would round the corner. Sometimes we would run along the tracks waving at the people who had somewhere to go, and sometimes we would just sit in the edge of the woods and watch that brown phantom with its front and back platforms and both a conductor and a motorman; and long, long down the sun-spotted car tracks the smiling, mustached conductor would lean over his ticket box and wave goodbye to his boyhood afternoons.

More than once we plotted to rob the trolley. We decided to lay a charge of dynamite on the tracks, wait until the car was over it, set it off, and then ride shouting and yelling out of the woods. That fact that we had neither horses nor dynamite hampered our plan, but, as boys will, we managed.

One day we put a whole roll of cap-pistol caps on the tracks, and then we hid in the woods and waited. Bobby, who had the caps, handed a roll to each of us, and we loaded up.

We heard the clang of the trolley bell, then at the Eastern Avenue end we saw it. It was a Holman Street car, and right up front talking to the motorman was the walrus-mustached conductor who had waved to us on his rare trips up the Eastern Avenue line. I felt my stomach knot; then the tears began to flow.

I jumped up and raced toward the tracks, waving my arms and screaming for the trolley to stop. The conductor and motorman, who had often made this out-of-the-way run through our boy-infested wood, smiled and waved back. At the last minute I tried to dive and knock the caps off the track, but the cowcatcher protecting the guide wheels of the car caught my arm and knocked me flat. I lay there dazed on the warm sun-spotted leaf mulch and waited for the trolley to lift off the tracks in a massive explosion.

There was, I think, a distinct sputter as the car's front wheels went over the caps, but through the noise of the wheels clattering along the uneven roadbed, I couldn't be sure.

The conductor, however, I remember. He must have run through the car. As I got up, he was standing with his big, blue-coated stomach pressed against the car's back railing. His face was red, and he waved his fist shouting, "Crazy damn kid! Crazy damn kid!" I had wanted to save his life, and now I was furious that he hadn't been blown sky high.

I was brushing leaves off my shirt and watching the car turn the corner onto Garrad Street when Billy and Bobby came running down out of the woods.

"Whoa, Lightning," said Billy as he pulled back hard on nothing.

"What happened, pardner?" asked Bobby as he danced about trying to gentle his imaginary steed, Blacky.

"Ah, why don't you guys grow up?" I said. "Let's play some baseball."

"OK I'll be Johnny Temple and Billy can be Ted Kluzewski."

"Great. I'll be Roy McMillan, but I can't throw too good. I hurt my arm sliding into second."

A Real Pickle

We all knew that Billy North was brave. After all, he once slipped out of the hollyhocks in my backyard, ran all the way down the alley, pushed through the side hedge, and beat on the window of the midgets' house. Ralph, who lived across the street and was the oldest kid on the block, told us that the midgets had a regular-sized brother who ran a restaurant and paid the midgets cash money for ground-up kids to make soup out of. Ralph said his uncle was eating in there once and found a finger in his soup. He said he nearly threw up.

Anyway, Bobby and I could hardly believe it when one afternoon we looked up, and here came Billy through the backyard with one of those garlic, dill pickles that cost a nickel.

"Where'd you get that?" I asked.

"Stole it," said Billy, who went to the movies at the Shirley a lot and liked to talk like a gangster.

"Sure you did," I said, and Bobby added, "Like hell." Bobby was always saying that. I thought it was neat, till I said it once at the supper table. Bobby, according to my mother, was "coming up with no more care than a weed." I wasn't too sure what that meant, but it somehow included the fact that I was never to say "like hell" again, ever.

"Yep. I stole it, punk."

"Where from?"

"Nielander's Saloon, punk."

"You ain't never been inside that saloon."

Bobby could say things like that because he was nearly as big as Billy, and besides, his mother wasn't always saying, "Now son, important people do not say 'ain't.'"

I just couldn't believe it. Billy had actually gone inside Nielander's Saloon. It wasn't really a saloon. Nielander's German Beer Garden, complete with swinging doors, sawdust floor, brass-railed bar, and lamp-lit patio, stood at the intersection where Twenty-first Street deadended into Garrad Avenue. Sometimes during the winter, on my way to the dairy, I peeked under the swinging doors into the dim, smoky interior, which seemed, night or day, to be filled with pipe-smoking old men drinking dark German beer from huge schooners and playing checkers. In the summer, as I passed the high wooden fence, between the slats I could see the same men smoking, drinking and playing nine pins. However much I might have wanted to go into Nielander's, I knew that if a boy my age set foot in a place like that he would, then and there, give his soul to the devil.

"You're going to Hell, Billy," I said, and I felt good because I used that word properly.

"Bet you won't steal one."

"Steal what?"

"Bet you won't steal a pickle, punk."

"Stealing is a sin."

"Oh yeh! You're a punk and a chicken too."

"Come on, Billy. Don't talk to him like that."

"Why not, Bobby-baby? You goin' to stop me? Is Bobby-baby goin' to take me on?" Billy shot a few quick jabs and laughed.

"I'll show you who's a chicken," I said. "Come on. I'll steal a pickle and one of them hard eggs too."

The three of us walked the short block from Maryland Avenue to Garrad in silence. Then Bobby said, "Let's go back."

"No. Chicken-punk here is goin'ta steal a pickle, ain't you?"

I didn't bother to answer him. I left them standing there, walked casually across the street, and quickly flattened myself against the front wall of Nielander's. I could hear the buzz of the neon Wiedemann's Beer sign in the window above me as I peeked in under the swinging door. No one was between me and the bar. All the old men were standing in a circle over in the corner watching a checker game wind up, so I slid under the door and started crawling through the sawdust toward the bar. I stood up slowly and reached into the pickle jar. It was then that I saw the egg jar was all the way down at the other end of the bar. I clutched the pickle and started crawling toward the eggs.

"Eh. Vas ist das?"

"Hey. It's a kid."

"Stop him."

I was up with the "Eh," but I was too far from the door.

"Zo you don't be happy to stealing von pikul. You cum back vor other von." The big German saloonkeeper bent my right arm up behind my back with one hand and pulled my left ear with the other one.

"I didn't steal your pickle!" I screamed.

"Zat's a vonny von. Mit der pikul in his hand he stands there and sez dat."

After considerably more twisting of both ear and arm, my name and address were established, and I was marched toward home in the custody of the saloonkeeper. As we went out the door, I noticed that neither Billy nor Bobby had stayed to see my triumph.

I stood in the kitchen while the saloonkeeper shouted to my father that he had "a cruke vor a zon." Finally he left, and my father came into the kitchen. He looked at me for a long time the way he always did when I wished that he would just go ahead and whip me and be done with it. Finally he said, "Well, son, you want to tell me about it?"

"It was Billy, sir. Billy made me do it."

"Well, Billy isn't my concern. I guess we'll have to settle this between the two of us," said Daddy. Then he grinned and said, “Son, it looks to me like you’ve gotten yourself into a real pickle.”

Billy and the Taft Newspaper

"This is really good," said Bobby, setting down his empty glass and eyeing the half-full lemonade pitcher with hope.

It was hot. The tall hollyhocks at the lower end of the backyard past the swing stood dead still. The only sounds were the low hum of the bumblebees among the red, purple, and pink blossoms of the hollyhocks and the click of ice as the heat melted it and it shifted in the glasses on the little picnic table we sat around.

"Would you like some more lemonade, Robert Taft?"

"Yes'm," said Bobby, but his face was twisted the way it always was whenever someone used his middle name. Bobby said when he grew up he was going to vote the straight Democratic ticket. He said that would teach his parents to give him a name like that. Mother said Bobby should be proud to be named for such a famous and honest man. Dad said that our town would be a sorry place without the Taft newspaper. He said that you could always depend on the *Times-Star* to lead the fight against the gangsters and that you couldn't even depend on the Scripp-Howard papers to wrap the garbage.

"Here you are, Robert Taft."

"Thank you'm."

"Would you like some more lemonade, James?"

"No."

"No what, James?"

"No'm."

"That's better. Well, what are you gentlemen planning to do this afternoon?"

Mother was always calling Bobby and me gentlemen. I guess she hoped somehow the thought would father the reality, but I always fought against any such transition. Bobby put down his empty glass for a third time.

"You know, Four-eyes..."

"Robert Taft, don't you call James that awful name."

"No'm. I mean, yes'm."

"That's all right, Robert Taft. You must learn not to call attention to others' infirmities."

"I was just going to say that I bet we..."

"Robert Taft. Surely you don't want me to tell your mother that you were over here this afternoon talking about gambling."

"No'm," said Bobby, looking more confused than usual. I knew what was up. I had used the phrase "I'll bet you" at the dinner table once. I guess you could say that I'd been there before. Mother finally let up on the sins of chance, and Bobby started again.

"We could probably sell a million dollars worth of lemonade out by the car stop when everyone comes home from work."

Mother, who had been gathering up the empty glasses, paused as she nearly always did whenever anyone mentioned the possibility of reaping an unreasonable profit.

"Wow, Robert Taft, a million dollars!" I exclaimed. I hated to do it, but calling him Bobby would have slowed things down and taken Mother out of her trance. "Could we do it, Mother? Huh? Could we?"

"What is it precisely that you wish to do?"

That stopped me. I turned to Bobby, who could usually be counted on to come up with a plan.

"Well, we could set up a lemonade stand by the fireplug. We could use the old desk out of the clubhouse and charge a nickel a glass. We could split the money fifty-fifty."

"How 'bout that, Mother? Could we? Huh? Could we?"

"Yes, James. I think that setting up a lemonade stand would be a fine way for you gentlemen to spend your afternoon."

We moved the desk out to the fireplug. Mother made up a fresh pitcher of lemonade and brought it and some old glasses out to us.

"You gentlemen be careful with that pitcher, you hear? That pitcher has been in this family since Heck was a pup."

"Yes'm."

Bobby and I arranged the glasses and put up a sign I'd made with black crayon on one of those pieces of cardboard the laundry put in Dad's shirts. Then we sat down on the curb and waited for the trolley cars to bring us our millions.

Several green and buff Eastern Avenue trolleys went past. Finally, a brown Holman Street car went by. Bobby and I waved to the motorman and the conductor, but no one got off. It was about four o'clock when Billy swaggered up.

"What you punks up to, Four-eyes?"

"James's mother said it isn't nice to call him that, Billy."

"Who asked you, Bobby-baby?"

"We're selling lemonade, Billy. Would you like some. It's only a nickel."

"No thanks, Four-eyes. I'm going for a swim in the river. Why don't you punks come with me?"

"No. We're going to make a million dollars."

"You ain't allowed in the river, are you Bobby-baby? Well, you punks go ahead and sit here in the sun. I'm going for a swim. There are easier ways to make money. See you punks in the funny papers."

"See ya, Billy."

Billy was right. Bobby wasn't allowed near the river and neither was I. After Billy went down the tracks, it seemed hotter. Between the rumblings of the trolleys, the only sounds were the hum of the step-down transformer on the light pole at the corner and the occasional ping of the expanding streetcar rails. Only the arrival of our first customer broke the sullenness of our mood.

"Five cents for a glass of lemonade, eh boys?"

"Yes sir, Mr. Johnson. It's good fresh lemonade. My mother just made it."

"And it's cold."

"Well, I'll just have me a glass of that. Then maybe my old woman won't be after me for drinking on my way home from work."

After Mr. Johnson had a second glass, there was a lull—then the deluge, and by five-thirty, when Billy came swaggering back up the tracks with his hair slicked back wet, Bobby and I were almost out of lemonade and we had two dollars and eighty cents.

"Hi, punks. How'd you do? You going to change your names to Nelson and Winthrop?"

"We made two dollars and eighty cents."

"Very good, Four-eyes. That makes my cut one dollar and forty cents. Hand it over."

"How come?" asked Bobby, who was fishing a quarter of a lemon out of the pitcher to eat.

"How come, Bobby-baby? I'll tell you 'How come!' Because if you don't I'll bust that big pretty pitcher, and then you would be out of the lemonade business. That's 'How come.'"

"Don't break that pitcher, Billy. My mother would kill me."

"OK Four-eyes. One dollar and forty cents."

"Give him the money, Bobby."

Bobby tossed the quarter of lemon back into the pitcher and pulled the money from the pocket of his shorts. He quickly divided it and held one handful out to Billy.

Billy took the handful of nickels, started up the tracks, and then turned toward us again.

"Say. You punks going to sell lemonade again tomorrow?"

"I don't think so, Billy."

"Suit yourself, Four-eyes. See ya, Bobby-baby."

Bobby and I split the remaining one dollar and forty cents. Then Bobby carried the desk back to the yard while I gathered up the pitcher and glasses.

"What do you want to do tomorrow, Four-eyes?"

"I don't know, Bobby."

"Well, see ya."

"G'night."

On the way into the house I tucked the *Times-Star* under my arm and carried it into the kitchen, where Mother and Dad were just sitting down to the table for supper.

"Wash your hands, James. We're ready to eat. Did you gentlemen have success with your lemonade business this afternoon?"

"Yes."

"Yes what, James?"

"Yes'm."

1990

The Sting

It was nearly the end of August, and so hot that people just sat around hating their shadows for being too close. I was sitting on the back steps in the shade of the big water maple, trying to think of something to do. In June, just after school was out, it seemed there would never be enough summer to do all the things I wanted to do. Now I'd done them all at least twice.

"Mother!" I yelled.

"Don't shout, James. I'm right here in the kitchen. What do you want?"

"Do I have to stay here in the backyard?"

"Can you keep from fighting with Robert Taft?"

"Yes'm." I didn't know if I could or not, but anything was better than sitting on the old porch steps watching my shadow melt.

"Well, I certainly hope you can, because one of these days Robert Taft or somebody else is going to cut you down to size."

I started to walk toward the gate. She added, "You hear?"

"Yes'm," I said. There was never any problem about hearing my mother. She was not one of those weak-voice, tiny women. She was big, and she was loud.

I said "Yes'm" because I knew she expected me to—not because I believed what she said about Bobby beating me up. Why, we'd had four fights that week, and I'd won them all. It wasn't that we didn't like each other. Bobby was my best friend. But it was hot and there just wasn't anything else to do.

I kicked through the dust-dry leaf mulch as I walked down the car tracks to Bobby's house. Bobby was sitting on the back porch.

"Hey, Four-eyes."

"Hey, Bobby. How's your eye?"

"It's okay, Four-eyes, but that was a lucky punch you got in. Even Billy says I was winning before that." It was a lucky punch. As bad as my eyes were, any punch I landed with my glasses off was a lucky punch. And Billy was right. Bobby had been bombing me before I stepped inside and clubbed him in the temple with a left hook.

"Where is Billy?" Billy could always think up something to do even on a hot day late in the summer.

"He went shopping with his grandmother to get some new clothes to start school."

"Boy, I'm glad I'm not Catholic like you guys," I said, sitting down beside Bobby on the back porch.

"Why?"

"Well, you and Billy always have to wear a white shirt and a tie to school."

"Yeh, but we get a lot of Saints' days off and you have to go to school."

"You mackerel snappers don't go to school much."

"Don't you call me a mackerel snapper, Four-eyes!" yelled Bobby, jumping up.

I got up and stuck my face right into his. "Why not? That's what you are."

"Am not."

"Are so."

"Am not."

"Are so."

"Boys. Boys. Boys," said Mrs. Taylor coming to the back screen door of her kitchen. Don't you have anything better to do than fight?" Not waiting for an answer, she moved back into the kitchen and said over her shoulder, "I sure will be glad when you boys go back to school."

"Bobby," I said after she was gone, "let's go see what's in Mr. Johnson's shed in the woods. Billy says he bets there's treasure or something in there."

"Old Man Johnson told us never to go near that shed, and besides, last week he told us to stay out of the woods till it rains, 'cause of fire."

"Oh come on, Bobby. He's at work. Besides, we'll just look in the shed."

"I don't know, Four-eyes"

"Just think what Billy will say when we tell him we know what old Johnson keeps in his shed."

"Oh, all right."

The shed was empty. It was a wooden cube maybe six feet on a side with some straw in it that smelled as if it had bedded an animal at some time. Nothing else—no secrets, no treasure, certainly nothing to tell Billy about. We were back where we started, in the heat with nothing to do.

"I know," said Bobby. "I'll be the sheriff and I'll lock you in the shed and you be one of the Dalton gang and try to escape."

"Neat," I said. Our only problem was that there wasn't any lock on the shed. Bobby solved this by closing the hasp and slipping an old stove bolt through the eye of the staple.

I tried the door, slamming my shoulder into it a few times. It held fast, and I was just getting ready to try to pry open one of the windows when I heard something, a high whizzing sound. Then I felt it, pain, a sting in my neck, a sting above the left eye. The shed was not empty. It was full of wasps, and my banging around had disturbed them.

"Bobby, let me out!" I screamed.

"You just settle down in there, Jack Dalton. The judge is out fishing this afternoon, but he'll be back in time to see that you're hanged by sunup."

"Ow! Bobby. No fooling. Let me out of here."

"Four-eyes, you ain't playing right."

"Bobby. There's wasps in here. Now let me out."

"You can't fool old Wyatt that way, Jack Dalton."

"Bobby, I'm going to kill you when I get out of here."

"That's better, Four-eyes. Just you carry on, Jack Dalton. We'll see how big you talk when the judge gets back."

By this time I'd been stung on the face maybe fifteen times, and it was clear to me that Bobby wasn't going to open the door. I didn't have time to pry open the window, so I just jumped through it. I landed on Bobby, who had come around to the side of the shed to see what I was screaming and carrying on about.

"God, Four-eyes. What happened to your face?"

Part of what happened was the small cut on my forehead that I had gotten when I went through the window, but most of what happened was the wasps. I didn't bother to explain; I just started pounding Bobby in the face with both fists. He defended himself briefly, but took the first opportunity to beat a retreat to his house.

I wandered back up the car tracks, my bloody face so swollen from the wasp stings that my eyes were nearly shut. My clothes were torn and dusty.

My mother foiled my attempt to sneak through the house to my room when she came into the dining room from the kitchen with a big platter of corn on the cob.

"James, you've been fighting again."

"Yes'm."

"With Robert Taft."

"Yes'm."

"Well, well. It looks as if he finally gave you just what you had coming. Go wash up for dinner, you hear?"

I wanted to tell her that I had pounded Bobby again, just like the other four times that week, but I didn't want to mention the wasps or the broken window or being in Mr. Johnsons's shed. So I just said "Yes'm" and went up to put some cold water on my face. The cold water felt good, 'cause it was sure hot.

Mending Wall

We were sitting around the kitchen table in the late October twilight. I was reading Dick Tracy in the *Times-Star*. Mother was hemming the vest to my George Washington costume, and my father was reading the *Meditations of Marcus Aurelius*.

"Says here, 'reasoning beings were created for one another's sake; that to be patient is a branch of justice, and that men sin without intending it.'"

"He never met James's friend, William," said Mother, looking up from her sewing.

Being George Washington was not my idea. The costume was a hand-me-down from my brother. I thought the white stockings made me look like a sissy, and I hated to think what Billy would say.

"What do you mean?" asked my father, although it had been more than a minute since Mother had said that about Billy. If you were going to talk to my father you had to get used to that. He would tune you out and go on reading or working, then suddenly, usually after you had gotten over being ignored, he would turn to you and answer your question in a quiet, even tone.

"I mean William plans most of his sinful acts carefully. I was just thinking perhaps William was created for Halloween. There," she said turning to me, "try this on for size."

I was always trying things on for size—pants being hemmed up, pants being let out a little.

"Stand up straight, James. How can I tell if the hem is even if you stand there like, ah, like..."

"Quasimodo. What do you mean Billy was created for Halloween, dear?"

"Well, he is constantly tearing up the neighborhood, breaking things, making a racket. It seems folks accept that sort of behavior out of boys on Halloween. But mind you, James, we will not tolerate it."

"Yes'm. Do I have to wear this ribbon on this wig?"

Mother didn't answer. She straightened the wig, stepped back toward the big cast metal stove, looked me over, and said, "My, but it seems such a short time since I sent your brother out in that costume. Here's your bag. Remember, ten o'clock."

"Yes'm."

"That's one Halloween I'll never forget," said my father, looking up from his book. I knew the story already, so I headed for the door.

When I got to the circle of light cast by the street lamp beside the car tracks, the gang was already there, gathered around Billy.

"Jeez, Four-eyes. What's that? We all agreed to dress as hobos."

"It belonged to my brother, and my mother made me wear it."

"Well, we ain't going to no dance, Four-eyes. At least take off that stupid hair and rub some dirt on those socks, or old Johnson'll see us."

I stuffed the wig into the honeysuckle bush and sat down on the rail of the car tracks. As I rubbed leaf mulch into the white stockings, Billy split the gang up and made plans to meet in the woods behind Mr. Johnson's house.

It was a beautiful dry wall stone fence. It ran along the back of Mr. Johnson's yard, dividing it from the woods. There were five of us. We worked quickly and quietly under Billy's direction. Finally there was not one stone on another. Then the whole yard lit up.

"Don't any of you move. I've got a shotgun."

We didn't move. I stood there shaking with the last stone still in my hand. As my eyes became accustomed to the light, I could see Mr. Johnson sitting on the second step of his back porch with a shotgun pointed at us.

"Took you boys just over an hour to take that wall down. Now we're going to see how long it takes you to put it back. Now get started."

There are dry wall stone fences all over Kentucky because there are rocks all over Kentucky. My father always said, "Kentucky would be the richest state in the Union if we could learn to eat rocks." The rocks work themselves up through the soil in the winter and are turned over during the spring plowing. Farmers toss the small ones and carry the larger ones to the field's edge.

In Kentucky they have been doing this forever, and when there were slaves in Kentucky and time to do this sort of thing, they piled the unwanted stones into long, low, beautiful fences that defined fields and stretched for miles along the narrow dusty pikes. Since they used no mortar, the craftsmen who constructed the dry wall fences had to develop an eye for the right stone to fit into the place they were working, the way my uncle could look at the pieces of the thousand-piece jigsaw puzzle I'd been working on for days and point to the very piece I needed next.

The trouble was, we weren't skilled slaves and we didn't have much time.

We worked as quickly as our fear would let us, but building a dry wall fence is an art hard to master. Three hours later all the stones were stacked again in a line along Mr. Johnson's backyard, but only the most lenient critic would have called it a wall.

"All right, boys, come here," said Mr. Johnson, standing up with the shotgun hip-leveled at us. We walked toward him in a bunch, each of us trying not to be in the front of the group. Finally we stood in the circle of the porch light less than a foot from the muzzle of the shotgun. Mr. Johnson set the gun aside and reached behind himself for something.

"Here you go. I want each of you to have an apple. Don't worry, I'm not going to tell your parents. I hope you learned something tonight. Happy Halloween, boys."

We each took an apple from the sack and thanked Mr. Johnson. He said good night to us, picked up his shotgun, walked into his house, and turned off the light.

With the light out and Mr. Johnson and his shotgun safely in the house, Nancy decided to set the record straight.

"We're not all boys," she shouted.

"Where have you been? It's nearly midnight. Where's your sack? Your wig? How did you get so dirty?" asked my father, looking up from his reading.

I rushed over and jumped into his lap, knocking his book to the floor, and buried my head against his shoulder.

"Father, I cannot tell a lie. That gang of boys from over on McCoy Street jumped me and took all my stuff."

My father held me close for a long time, stroked my hair, then said, "At least you weren't hurt. When your brother wore that outfit on Halloween, they broke his leg trying to stuff him into a storm sewer."

Cinder Hill

In my hometown, Covington, Kentucky, it didn't snow often enough for anyone to get used to it. My father said that it had snowed more when he was a kid. Although he had never walked five miles through the snow to school, he had driven a Model A Ford over the three star routes out of Brooksville as a substitute mailman, and he had numerous stories about icy skids on frozen dirt roads.

Our snows just didn't measure up to the snows of my father's youth, but every time it did snow, everybody went crazy. All the adults talked about how cold it was and about how hard it was to get around. All the kids (except for the Catholics who never went to school anyway because of Saint This-and-that Day and who always got out when it even rained hard) squirmed in their seats and waited for the bell to release them in a mad dash for their sleds.

The best place to slide was a street up near the high school that had developed the name "Cinder Hill" from the former practice of tossing coal cinders on it in an attempt to improve the traction. It had never worked, and by the time I was a boy, the city merely closed Cinder Hill to traffic by placing sawhorses at the top and bottom.

When a snow fell on a Saturday (which seemed almost never), Cinder Hill sprouted kids with sleds. Billy and I always tried to be among the first on the hill. Although I didn't like sharing my sled with Billy, he was big enough to make sure that no one else ever took it, and half the turns were better than none.

"Hey, let me have a turn, Four-eyes," said a big McCoy Street kid who had "borrowed" my sled before.

"Get your hands offa that sled, punk," snarled Billy.

"Sure, Billy. I just thought the kid was standin' there. I thought somebody ought to use the sled."

"Well, somebody is goin' to, punk. Me."

The brief ride down the ice-covered hill was always followed by the long walk back up. Boys who didn't have sleds gathered on the sidewalk on both sides to pelt the sledders with snowballs. The boys going down hill, braced by the exhilaration of their speed, laughed when the snowballs shattered against their hands, spraying their faces with icy shards. The boys dragging their sleds back up the hill were sad, almost sitting targets. Many of the younger boys were driven from the hill by the gauntlet of sledless warriors.

We were generally too busy to notice the cold. It first attacked exposed noses and lips, then feet and hands, until toward evening, our hearts, warm with the excitement of the day, and our stomachs, totally empty and crying to be fed, were the only organs untouched by the cold.

My father had never sledded on Cinder Hill. "That's no hill at all, boy," he said. "When I was a boy, we slid the Depot Hill in Brooksville from the center of town past the Jett Place to the Depot where the spur line ended. My sled was no Flexible Flyer. It was a homemade wooden sled with steel band runners. There was no way I could turn it. I just got on and flew in a straight line."

At the bottom of Cinder Hill, after a short flat run, sledders had to cut right or left to avoid going out into a busy street which, because it was a trolley route, had traffic on it even in the worst weather.

That trolley line at the bottom of Cinder Hill always bothered me because of my father's favorite story. "This one time I was roaring down Depot Hill on a glaze of ice, and the freight wagon turned the corner and started up the hill, team of six. Like I told you, I couldn't turn. The teamster was screaming at me, standing up with six reins in his left hand and a twelve-foot whip in his right hand, and he popped me twice with that whip as I zipped right straight down under the singletree with three horses on each side of me. He popped me again when I came out from under the back of the wagon, tore my coat right off me with that big black snake whip."

Late one Saturday afternoon, after each of us had had a hundred or so trips down the hill and it was again Billy's turn, he smiled at me and said, "How 'bout goin' down together? I'll steer. You lay on top of me piggyback bellybuster." I couldn't believe it. Billy was asking me to slide Cinder Hill with him.

"What about it, punk? Want to go?"

"Sure, Billy. What do you want me to do?"

"Don't do nothin'. Just lay on my back and Ol' Billy'll give you a ride you won't forget."

I could feel our slow start, but soon the added weight of the two of us began to tell and the sled began to pick up speed. I could see only blurs as we zoomed past the boys trudging back up the hill dragging their sleds. The boys on the sidewalks had no chance. They were used to slower moving targets, and their snowballs fell harmlessly behind us.

The sound of the wind screaming in my ears was cut suddenly by another sound, the clanging of a trolley bell. As we reached the bottom and started across the short run, Billy tried to turn the sled, but our speed was too great. "Can't turn, punk," said Billy as we slid closer to the trolley tracks. At ten feet and closing, even though the streetcar had its brakes on full, I knew we were dead. I shut my eyes and waited. There was a great noise of grinding metal as we bumped up on the tracks and passed right under the trolley car just behind the front wheels. We barely cleared the rear wheels on the other side, ran up over the curb, and crashed into a snow-covered hedge.

The snow from the hedge filtered down my collar onto my flushed neck as I rolled off the sled. Billy was just lying there laughing and laughing.

"Shit," he finally said. "She-it. I told you I'd give you a ride you'd remember, punk."

Being Close to the Front

It was a late fall Saturday, too late to care about baseball and too early to hope for snow. We were in the woods near the stubbled remains of Mr. Johnson's small stand of sweet corn, with nothing to do.

"Well, what do you guys want to do?" asked Bobby.

"I don't know. What do you want to do, Billy?"

"Look at this," said Billy, pulling a corn stubble out of the ground, roots and all. "Bet I can hit the car tracks from here."

Billy leaned back and arced the corn stubble high into the air toward the car tracks. It smashed into the branches of an oak tree high above the cut the trolleys ran through between their uptown run on Eastern Avenue and their return trip to Cincinnati down Garrad Street. Dirt and twigs rained down.

"Didn't make it," I said.

"Would have!"

"Bet I can hit Mr. Johnson's shed."

"Of course you can, Bobby. Anyone could hit the shed from here."

"Four-eyes couldn't. He can't see the shed from here."

"Can too."

"I know," said Bobby. "Let's go over on Eastern and lob these into the street like hand grenades. See, like this. You got to keep your arm straight and count to three after you pull the pin; then you let it go."

"Neat," said Billy. "Cars can be jeeps and trucks can be tanks and the trolley..."

"I don't think we should throw things at cars."

"What's the matter, Bobby? Are you chicken? Bobby's chicken, Four-eyes."

"You guys do what you want to. I'm going home."

"We could do something else, Bobby. Don't go."

"Aw, let the chicken go. Come on, Four-eyes, grab some of these grenades and follow me. Silent maneuvers."

Bobby walked down the bank from the woods, across his backyard, and up the stairs to his house. I gathered up an armful of corn stubble and followed Billy's "advance" hand signal.

Billy and I crossed the car tracks and climbed the embankment to the empty lot overlooking Eastern Avenue. There, prone in the dried out ragweed and Queen Anne's Lace, Billy went through a series of incomprehensible gestures. I shook my head to show I didn't understand, and he repeated the gestures. I shook my head again.

"Jeez, I hate to break silence, but you are so stupid."

"I'm stupid? You look like you've got ants in your pants. What is all that supposed to mean?"

"You can't look, punk. You have to stay down and lob the grenades," Billy snarled.

"Why?"

"Because of the machine gun fire. Jeez, you're stupid."

"Why didn't you just say so?"

"Because they'll hear us. No one has ever been this close to the lines."

I started to reply, but Billy cut me off with the "silence" sign. Then he counted to three and arced a corn stubble high into the air in the general direction of Eastern Avenue.

"Ka-boom," he yelled and then pointed to me.

I gripped the stubble and whispered, "One. Two. Three," before I let it go into a slow curve. I was all ready to make an impact and explosion sound when I heard a thud and the screech of tires.

In spite of machine gun fire, I stuck my head up and looked down onto the street. A man was getting out of a black

Ford sedan and looking at his windshield, which was covered with dirt.

"Jeez, Four-eyes, you hit that guy's car."

I expected Billy to tell me to get my head down or give me the silent signal for rapid retreat. Instead he yelled, "Run for it," and headed down the embankment toward the tracks.

When Billy yelled, the man looked up and saw me staring down at him.

"Hey, kid! You! Stop!"

Given the choice between his command and Billy's, I chose Billy's and caught up to him before he got halfway up the tracks toward Maryland Avenue.

"What are we going to do, Four-eyes? He's after us."

Billy was right. The man was following us, but he was fat and slow.

"We'll hide under the front porch. He won't find us there."

We slipped under my porch and stared through the lathwork at the car tracks. The man appeared and looked down Maryland. He walked slowly down the other side of the street, looking everywhere.

"He'll see us."

"Quiet, Billy. He can't see us here."

I hoped I was right. He paused right in front of our house and stared right at us. Then he went on back down the tracks.

"He's gone."

"Wait, Billy. He might come back. We better stay here for awhile."

We sat and played Stretch with Billy's Barlow in the cool earth underneath the porch. Since the object of Stretch was to stick a jack knife in the ground and see if your opponent could stretch out, touch the knife with his foot, and then pull it from the ground and stick it for you to try to stretch to, it was a bit odd playing it under the porch where we couldn't even stand up.

"He's gone. Let's go."

"No, wait. Here, see if you can reach this," I said as I flipped the knife in the dark earth about two and a half feet from Billy.

"That's easy," Billy said. "Stretch is no fun in here. You can't stand up. Let's..."

I assume Billy was going to say, "Go," but instead he gave me the secret hand signal for silence and pointed through the lathwork toward the curb.

He didn't need to signal. When I saw the police car at the curb in front of my house, I could barely breathe, much less say anything. A tall thin policeman got out of the passenger's side and walked straight up my walk and up the porch stairs. His partner, shorter and stockier, went up the stairs of the house across the street.

We could hear the tall policeman walk across the porch and knock. My mother answered the door.

"Good afternoon, Officer."

"Ma'am, I'm Officer Goodrich. We've had a complaint about kids, two boys, throwing things at cars over on Eastern. A motorist chased them over here, but lost sight of them."

"Two boys, you say?"

"Yes ma'am. That's all he said, 'two boys.' No description. Nothing. I wonder if you could tell me about the boys in the neighborhood, which ones would be likely to be involved in this sort of thing."

"Well, there's Billy North over on Garrad Street. He's coming up like a weed. I don't allow my son to have anything to do with him. If I were you, Officer, I would start there."

"Where is your son today, Ma'am?"

"He's out playing somewhere. But I assure you, Officer, my son is a young gentleman. He would never be involved in anything like this."

"I hope not, Ma'am. This is serious business. That motorist could have had a wreck or worse. Well, I'll go over on Garrad and talk to the Norths. Which house is it?"

"Last house on the other side of the street right where the tracks turn. But no one's home. That's probably why the boy is the way he is."

"Well, thank you, Ma'am. Good day."

"Good day, Officer."

He walked back across the porch, down the steps to the sidewalk, and around the corner into the alley towards Garrad Street.

We slid out from under the porch and crouched against the house next to the coal chute.

"What are we going to do, Four-eyes? The cops are after us."

"Calm down, Billy. They aren't after you. You didn't do anything. Besides, you heard the cop. They don't have a description."

"You think your mother needs a description? You heard her. Right off, she tells him I was probably involved."

"No one's home at your place."

"No, not now, but I know my old man will beat me for this. He hates cops. He don't want cops around, ever. And I bet your mother knows who the second kid is, too."

Billy was right. My mother knew, and I knew I had to come up with a distraction or I was really going to catch it. The outside faucet saved me. Dad had already taken the hoses in to keep them from freezing, but he hadn't turned the outside faucet off yet.

"Here," I said turning the faucet on. "Put your head under this."

"What?"

"Don't ask me, just do it."

Billy put his head under and I quickly did the same. The air was cool enough to make me realize that my cover story was at best improbable, but I had to try it.

With hand signals, I motioned Billy back out to the corner of the car tracks. As we started towards my house again, the tall cop, who was coming from Garrad Street, shouted.

"You, boys, stop."

"Jeez, Four-eyes, now what?"

"Don't worry, Billy. I can handle this."

We stopped. The tall cop continued to walk toward us. By the time he reached us on the sidewalk in front of Nancy's house, my mother was on the porch wearing a sweater over her apron with her arms folded against the chill.

"You boys been over on Eastern Avenue?"

"We crossed Eastern," I said. "We've been down swimming in the Licking River."

"Swimming in the Licking River!" my mother screamed. "You get in this house right now. I've told you never to go near that river, and I've told you not to have anything to do with that boy." She pointed at Billy.

Our wet heads and my mother's reaction took the cop completely by surprise. Billy headed for his house, and I walked slowly past my mother.

"Just a moment, Ma'am. I'd like to ask your son if he saw anything unusual over on Eastern."

"Officer, I told you before, my son would have nothing to do with throwing anything at automobiles. And I assure you, right now he wishes he were the guilty party."

My mother was wrong there. I had been warned since the time I was allowed to leave the yard never to go near the river. But I knew that putting myself in personal danger would not raise my father's wrath as much as my damaging property, endangering someone else's life, and bringing the police into his living room. I was satisfied with my choice, but my mother went on predicting dire things that almost made me wonder.

"There is nothing you could do to him in prison that his father won't do to him when he hears about this. Swimming in the river in the last week of October! He'll probably catch cold and die. It would serve him right."

Smelling the Ozone, Up Close and Personal

"It will be easy," said Billy. "I saw some of the McCoy Street gang do it last week."

We were sitting under a tree in Mr. Johnson's woods, and Billy was explaining how we could go about pulling a trolley pole off the overhead electric wire.

"They hid in the grape arbor of the beer garden down by Nielander's saloon, and when the trolley came past, they ran behind it, jumped up, and grabbed the guide wire on the pole, and swung across behind the trolley. There were sparks everywhere, and that trolley stopped dead."

"What happened then?" Bobby asked.

"What do you think happened then, Bobby-baby? The motorman came off the front of the trolley screaming, and they ran through the vacant lot on the other side of Nielander's back to McCoy Street."

"Those cars go pretty fast," I said, stripping bark from a twig.

"Thirty-five miles an hour on that long run down Greenup Street," said Billy.

"How are we going to run behind something going thirty-five miles per hour and grab it?"

"We aren't, Four-eyes. We'll catch it right here at the head of the woods just after it turns off Eastern Avenue and stops. It's never going fast through here."

"I don't know," said Bobby. "It sounds dangerous. My father says there are 600 volts of electricity in that overhead line."

"I think Bobby's right," I said. "Have you ever seen the sparks when the trolley jumps its wire up at the corner of Twentieth and Greenup in front of Schulte and Wisher's? Blue smoke and sparks everywhere and a real funny smell in the air."

"That's ozone," said Bobby. "My father says that you can smell the same thing in the air right after a lightning strike, if you're close enough. You know. You see the flash and hear the crack and rumble almost together. Then you smell the ozone."

"I found out all I ever wanted to know about electricity when I stuck the aerial wire from our radio into a floor plug," I said, tossing the smooth twig aside.

"What happened?"

"What do you think happened, Bobby? I was killed."

"No, what really happened?"

"It knocked me all the way across the living room and put a lump on my head."

"Did you smell the ozone?"

"I don't know, Bobby. But I'll tell you, I don't want to mess with 600 volts if 120 can leave a knot on my head."

"Electricity can't put a knot on your head," said Bobby, frowning. "It can turn you green, but it can't put a knot on your head."

"Turn you green?" said Billy. "How can it turn you green?"

"I don't know. But my father said he knew a man once, was a lineman, touched a high voltage power line, and it turned him green. After that he couldn't work on nothing. People used to see him walking the back roads at night. Called him The Green Man."

"I heard of him," said Billy.

"Well, I don't want to be green," I said, "any more than I want a knot on my head."

"We won't be anywhere near the power line. We'll grab the guide wire and pull the trolley off," said Billy.

"You can grab that line if you want to," I said. "I'm not having a thing to do with it."

Part of my reluctance was the experience I had had with electricity, but part of it was my love of the trolleys. The Green Line—which is what everybody called The Covington, Newport and Cincinnati Street Railway because the cars that crossed the Ohio River into Northern Kentucky were painted green—had ten routes on its schedule:

1 Ft. Mitchell
2 Greenup (rush hour only)
4 Main Street
5 Holman
8 Eastern Avenue
9 Covington-Newport
#10 Lewisburg (rush hour only)
#11 Ft. Thomas
#14 York Street
#16 Washington Avenue (rush hour only)

By the time I was old enough to love trolleys the #3 Ludow, #6 Rosedale, and #7 Latonia had been converted to trolley bus lines. Even worse, the #12 Bellevue-Dayton, #13 South Bellevue, and #15 Southgate had been converted to gas buses.

I had memorized the routes from a map I had cut out of the *Times-Star* and pinned to the wall over my bed. I was determined to ride every mile of those trolley routes someday.

I rode the #8 Eastern Avenue when my mother and I went shopping at Coppin's Department Store. The #8's big green and buff cars were the ones that ran the two-block car track from Eastern Avenue past the dead end of Maryland Avenue, where I lived, to Garrad Street.

The car tracks were the southern terminus of the #8 line. Here the southbound trolleys turned north again toward Cincinnati's Dixie terminal.

I had also ridden the shorter brown and white Holman Street cars, and once during the war, when there was no gas for the car, my parents and I took the #8, transferred to a #1 Ft. Mitchell, and walked from Park Hills Station to Devou Park for a picnic and a band concert that was given to help raise money for the USO. After the concert, we boarded another trolley at the Park Hills Station and my father introduced me to Ray Householder, the motorman, who had been operating cars longer than anyone else for the Green Line. His hair was white, and his face was lined with years. But his eyes were bright as he told us of some of his experiences running the trolleys.

"The best times of all," he reminisced, "were the runs through the woods on a warm autumn evening. There were no autos to worry about on the private right-of-way, and it was mighty nice to see all the fall colors in the rays of the setting sun. With the front windows open, the fresh air flowed through the car better than any air-conditioner could do it."

"A trolley sounds different running through a woods than it does on the city streets," he continued. "A softer sound comes from the motors because the earth and the trees absorb it, and then there is the clickety-clack of the wheels on the rail joints that sets a sort of tune with the gentle rocking of the car—ah, that's the life for me," he uttered, as his voice dropped off and his eyes looked dreamy and deep.

I found myself dreaming too, dreaming of standing at the controls of my own trolley car, running through the woods on a warm autumn evening. I knew, at that moment riding back on the Ft. Mitchell line from a picnic in Devou Park, I wanted to be a trolley motorman someday.

Billy wanted something else. He wanted to emulate the derring-do of the infamous McCoy Street gang.

"Well, you punks can suit yourselves. I'm going to dewire the next trolley that comes into these woods."

Billy did just what he said he would. He waited in the woods till the #8 car started slowly away from its stop after turning the corner from Eastern Avenue. Then he darted down the embankment, ran behind the car, grabbed the guide wire on the trolley, and swung to the other side of the car.

The trolley stopped dead. The motorman got off and ran toward the rear of the car in time to see Billy disappearing down the side street by Wiemann's Store, heading for the river. The motorman scanned the woods, looking straight at us once, but Bobby and I were concealed in some high grass, and he did not see us. Finally he quit searching the area for the malefactor and pulled the guide to put the trolley back on its wire.

When the trolley pulled away toward its turn onto Garrad Street, I snuck a look at Bobby, whose face was deep bluish green color. I realized that I had been holding my breath since Billy ran down the bank toward the trolley.

"Jeez, Bobby," I exhaled, "you look just like the Green Man."

"Four-eyes, I thought for sure that motorman saw us. I thought we were done for."

The motorman didn't catch us. Billy eventually tired of recounting his bravery, and by late August the incident was pretty well forgotten.

One day I was walking down the car tracks toward Eastern when a #8 came around the corner and stopped at the wide concrete sidewalk that constituted the trolley stop. The motorman tossed his hat aside, slapped his changer with his palm, swung down the steps from the car, and went across Eastern Avenue to Wiemann's Store. It was a very hot day, very muggy. Thunder rumbled in the distance. A storm was imminent. I guess the motorman was heading to Wiemann's for a cold drink of pop. I could understand that. That is where I was heading with a bag full of empty pop bottles worth two cents apiece.

Pop bottles were a source of extra money. Any bottle you could find was worth two cents, and people tossed them aside when they were empty, so at the beginning of summer they were plentiful. As the summer wore on, the empties were rarer. But the rack by the pop machine in the basement of St. Elizabeth's Hospital, down on Twenty-first Street, a block from my house, had a nearly endless supply. Late in the summer, whenever I needed a little money, I got a paper bag and went to the hospital to make my rounds. My parents wanted me to turn the pop bottles into pennies, save the pennies till I had a quarter, turn the quarter into a savings stamp, and keep buying stamps till I had enough for a government savings bond. I was interested in more immediate rewards. So I generally headed straight for Wiemann's to collect on my effort.

Just as I passed the trolley, the air compressor throbbed to life and made that big green and buff trolley more interesting than a cold drink.

I put my sack of bottles down and scampered up the steps onto the trolley. The car was empty. The motorman's hat was on his seat next to the fare box. And although he had taken his coin changer with him, he had left his direction key and air brake handle in place.

I took a glance out the window toward Wiemann's. The motorman was not in sight, so I decided to chance putting on his hat. It was way too big. It slid down over my eyes so that the bill touched my nose. But with the air compressor shaking the slotted floorboards beneath my feet, I could almost feel the clack and sway of the trolley responding to my command. Almost.

I took the hat off, hung it on the fare box, and glanced again toward Wiemann's. No one.

I pushed in on the brake pedal as far down as I could, released the dead man control. I sat down on the motorman's' chair, shut the trolley doors, pushed the direction key forward, slid the controller slowly clockwise, and moved the trolley smoothly up the track toward my house before I realized I had left my bag of empties at the trolley stop. I didn't know I knew how to drive a trolley, but I guess all those times I had sat and watched every move the motorman made helped. It was easy.

Mr. Johnson was waiting at the trolley stop on my street, but I didn't stop for him. He was so surprised he didn't look up at the trolley till I was past him.

I enjoyed the rock and sway of the moving car as it clicked along the car track toward Garrad Street. I turned the controller counterclockwise to reduce my speed as I approached the turn onto Garrad Street. I was wishing Billy and Bobby were with me because they would have loved it. Then I saw Billy coming out of his house at the top of Garrad Street. I hit the floor pedal and rang the trolley bell twice.

As I rotated the controller and picked up speed heading down Garrad Street, I saw Billy's face fall open in a slack-jawed stare. I breezed past more amazed trolley passengers by Nielander's and slowed for the corner onto Twentieth Street. Then I speeded up past Summe and Rattermann's dairy and Louie Martz's shoe shop and past more potential customers. Dark clouds scudded overhead.

As I turned the corner of Twentieth and Greenup in front on Schulte and Wisher's, the trolley pole jumped its wire in a green and blue flash of electricity, and the green and buff car came to a halt. I opened the door, jumped down, hit the ground running through the strange odor of ozone, and ducked into the passageway between Schulte and Wisher's and the big red brick Victorian office building next to it.

From the security of the passageway, I watched as Billy and a breathless group of trolley passengers, led by the angry and winded motorman, stormed around the corner and approached the stalled trolley.

The motorman mounted the steps. "Empty," he said. "Whoever it was, he's gone."

"Call the police," one of the passengers said angrily.

"If we do that," another one said, "we'll have to wait around forever. I need to get to work."

"Did anyone see the thief?" asked the motorman, putting on his hat.

"I did," a passenger called. "He was short."

"He was black," said another.

"No he wasn't," said a third.

"Wasn't what?" asked the motorman. "Wasn't short or wasn't black?"

"Wasn't black," said the third passenger.

"Yes, he was," the second passenger insisted.

"This is pointless," said the motorman. "You all get on this trolley. I'll put the pole back on the wire and we'll go to Cincinnati."

The motorman put the trolley back on the wire, and the crowd of passengers piled on and paid their fares; the trolley rolled away, and I joined Billy in front of Schulte and Wisher's.

"Jeez, Four-eyes, you stole a trolley. The McCoy Street Gang never stole a trolley. You're lucky they didn't catch you. What do you think they would do to you if they caught you stealing a trolley?"

"I don't want to think about it. It's hot, Billy. Let's go down to the hospital for some empties and get us a cold pop."

The storm that had been threatening all afternoon broke with a tremendous flash of lightning above the hospital. A crack of thunder followed immediately and shook the windows of the dairy. We ran in a downpour from the dairy to the basement of the hospital through the smell of ozone.

"Jeez, Four-eyes, that smell is that ozone Bobby told us about. That was close."

"Too close, Billy. Much too close."

Fireworks

It was the end of June, but cold enough to wear a jacket. We'd been out of school for a month, and already time was beginning to drag. But pretty soon it would be July Fourth. My mom and dad and I would go to the ballpark and watch the two local brewery-sponsored softball teams play an exhibition doubleheader against some teams from Lexington or Louisville. After the game, we would watch the community fireworks display. I loved the fireworks at the ballpark because I wasn't allowed to shoot off firecrackers on the Fourth.

"What are you doin' on the Fourth, Bobby?"

"Same ol' stuff. Go to the ballpark. Watch the Keggers and the Brewers. I guess stay for the fireworks."

"Yeh, me too. I wish I had some real fireworks."

We were standing by my back fence, where we stood when we didn't have anything else to do and wished our lives were different and wonderful and exciting, which was most of the time.

"Here comes Billy. Maybe he knows where we could get some fireworks."

Billy came cantering up on his horse, Ranger. He reined him in, dismounted, and came toward us in a rolling stride.

"What are you cowpokes up to? You want to ride out and rustle some cattle or knock over a bank?"

We all had horses, not real horses, but the best horses we could imagine. I had Flash. Bobby's horse was Blacky.

Although robbing a bank held some appeal, that day we were more interested in fireworks.

"Naw, Billy. We want to get some fireworks. Do you know where we can get some?"

"Sure, Four-eyes," he said, reaching into the pocket of his green jacket. "Here." He held his hand out with a palm full of Ladyfingers in it.

"Where did you get them, Billy?"

"My ol' man got them in Tennessee. You can buy all kinds of fireworks in Tennessee."

"Are you going to shoot them off?"

"Naw, Bobby, I thought I'd smoke some of them. Of course I'm going to shoot them off. That's what fireworks are for."

"I'm not allowed to have fireworks. My father says that they're dangerous. You can get your hand blown off or lose an eye with those things."

"I'm not surprised, Bobby. What about you, Four-eyes? You got any fireworks?"

"I got some sparklers and some snakes."

"Sparklers and snakes are kids' stuff. Look at these." He pulled three one-inchers and a cherry bomb from his pocket.

"What's that?"

"It's a cherry bomb, Bobby, and my ol' man says one of these will blow a mailbox right off its post. He did it once when he was a kid. Blew up his neighbor's mailbox and never did pay for it."

"That's great, Billy, but there aren't any mailboxes here in town."

"Sure there are, Bobby. There's a mailbox on every house," I said. And some houses have mail slots. We could light one and slip it through the mail slot and ka-boom!'"

"Sounds like trouble to me, Four-eyes. You know you manage to get in trouble almost every time you do something with Billy."

"We're not going to get in trouble, Bobby-baby. We're just going to blow up the midgets' mailbox."

"The midgets. I'm not going near the midgets' house. You remember what Ralph said about them and their brother." The midgets were supposed to have a regular-sized brother in Cincinnati who paid them cash money for ground-up kids to make soup out of.

"Nothing like that is going to happen to us because we won't get caught. We can sneak around the hedge, up the front steps, slip this sucker in the mailbox, and be gone by the time it blows. What do you say, Four-eyes? Want to blow up a mailbox?"

"Sure, Billy. What about it, Bobby?"

"Well, I guess. But I'm only going to the hedge."

We went down the alley and around the hedge and stopped by the front walk. Billy turned to Bobby and asked him if he had a match. That was funny. Billy was the only one of us who ever smoked and the only one who ever carried matches.

"Must have left them in my other pants," said Bobby.

"Right, Bobby. You're a big help in this mailbox-blowing business. Lucky I happen to have a match." Billy whipped a wooden kitchen match out of his hip pocket. "Let's go, Four-eyes."

When we got to the porch, Billy struck the match with his thumbnail, lit the cherry bomb, and stuffed it into the midgets' mailbox, which was already full of mail. Just before we ran off the porch, I had an inspiration. I reached out and pushed the midgets' doorbell.

Things happened in a hurry. As we left the porch, Billy fell and I tripped over him. We were lying face down on the midgets' sidewalk when the door opened and one of the brothers came out and yelled.

"What the hell are you kids doing on my porch?"

Just then the mailbox exploded with the loudest sound I had ever heard. The front of the box blew straight over Billy and me and came within inches of Bobby, who was standing by the hedge watching the midget roll around on the front porch holding his ears and moaning as fragments of mail floated on top of him.

He was still down when Billy and I shot past Bobby and headed for the alley.

Bobby caught up with us as we turned through the gate into the sanctuary of my backyard.

"Boy," said Bobby, "we're in trouble now."

"Naw," said Billy, "we're immortal now. That sack of shit the McCoy Street Gang lit on the midgets' porch last Halloween is nothing. That midget will never be able to tell anyone who did it, and it was the best. We really got the midgets this time. Four-eyes ringing that bell was terrific. What did he look like when it went off, Bobby?"

"He looked like a short deaf man with pieces of mail all over him. Do you think that was the same one that stomped out the burning sack of shit?"

"Who knows? All midgets look alike, to me, but we better not stay here. He might get up and follow us."

"You're right, Four-eyes. What do you want to do now?"

"Let's go to the woods, Billy, and set off the rest. Maybe we can launch some tin cans."

"OK, punks, let's."

We went up our back walk past the hollyhocks, the swing set, the sandbox and the two big maple trees, through the gate, and down the walk in our side yard to Maryland Avenue. We talked the whole way about what we had just done and how we would be legends like the McCoy Street Gang. When we got to the front of my house a scissors grinder's horse and wagon was ground-hitched in front of Mr. Johnson's house.

A scissors grinder came around a couple times a year to sharpen scissors and knives and tools. Scissors grinders sold scissors and knives, but no one on our street ever bought any. My father said if you buy good tools and take care of them, they'll last a lifetime and then some. He never said what you did with tools after you died.

The scissors grinder carried a small treadle grinding wheel in his wagon, and people brought their dull implements to the curb whenever they heard his street cry.

Scissors Grinder
Knife man
Bring me your tools

Scissors Grinder
Knife man
Bring me your tools

Mrs. Johnson in her old black sweater, her arms folded over a purple floursack apron, stood at the back of the wagon. A spray of sparks erupted from the grinding wheel as the grinder sharpened her kitchen knives.

We stopped to watch the shower of sparks. It wasn't much in the way of fireworks, but every little thing could quickly become fascinating on a street as dull as Maryland Avenue.

"Look, Four-eyes. That looks like that fountain of fire they set off at the ballpark last year."

"Bobby, you're crazy. That's just sparks. If you want to see fireworks, watch this."

Billy struck another match, lit a one-incher, and tossed it under the scissors man's horse.

I couldn't believe it. I stood there dumbfounded, watching the fuse burn down and waiting for the one-incher to explode and panic the horse, stampeding the wagon up the street onto the car tracks. I could see the scissors grinder and his grindstone falling out the back on top of Mrs. Johnson. I could see the frightened horse bumping the wagon over the ties of the trolley track straight for the oncoming trolley with the motorman desperately clanging his bell. I pictured the awful crash and screams of the horse, and the splintering of the wagon and the terrible groan as the trolley canted up on two wheels and slowly tipped over on its side.

The explosion was quite loud. All three of us jumped, but the horse just kept on snuffing around in his nose bag of oats. He didn't respond at all.

The horse didn't respond, but the scissors grinder whipped around the back of the wagon with a freshly sharpened knife in his hand long enough to row a boat with.

"If one inch of you move, I cut you top to bottom." He waved the knife slowly left to right. With the horse chomping oats behind us and that immense knife in front of us, we didn't move an inch.

"What you do to my horse? Show me."

Billy reached in his pocket and held our the two remaining one-inchers.

"Firecrackers. You threw firecrackers at my poor horse to scare him. But he didn't move. He's deaf. He was in the war, carried ammunition, the big guns. He can't hear thunder. So you cruel little bastards didn't get to have any fun. How about if I cut you up into pieces? Would that be fun?"

"Please, mister, we didn't mean anything. We just had these fireworks for the Fourth, and..." I didn't know what to say next. We had just missed getting cut up for soup by the midgets, and here we were facing the scissors man's knife.

"For the Fourth?" He spat on the ground at our feet. "You don't even know what this country is about. What do you know about Independence? And freedom. This old horse fought for this country, and you cruel little bastards come along..."

"Were you in the war too, mister?" I asked. I didn't really care one way or another, but I figured we were better off if this angry scissors man with his long knife was talking about something other than what cruel little bastards we were.

"Yeh, you could say. See?" He rolled the sleeve of his shirt up to expose the forearm of the hand that held the knife. There on the inside of his forearm was a long series of tiny blue numbers. There must have been ten of them. "There are my numbers. I was in the war, and I survived. This old horse was in the war, and he survived. We got together when I bought him at an auction. He doesn't hold it against me that I survived. He just pulls my wagon, and I am free in this country to sharpen knives and try to forget."

He was crying now. I had never seen a grown man cry. His tears rolled down his face and off his chin and soaked into his red and green striped shirt. "Try to forget this cruelty," he said, lowering the knife. "Excuse, please. The worst thing that could happen would be to become like them. Go on." He handed the two one-inchers back to Billy. "Go on and enjoy your firecrackers, but please, boys, don't be evil. There is enough evil in this world."

He rolled his sleeve back down, buttoned the cuff, and walked back to Mrs. Johnson who was standing on the curb with her hands pressed to her mouth.

"I think this will hold for a while," he said, handing her the knife. "Try not to get it wet. Water dulls a knife. Just wipe it dry every time."

I reached out and patted the deaf horse on its neck. It pulled its nose out of its feed bag and looked at me.

"You guys want to go to the woods?" I asked.

"Naw," said Billy. "I'm going home."

"Me too," said Bobby.

"You want these, Four-eyes?" asked Billy, holding out the firecrackers.

"No. I have some sparklers and some snakes."

Making a Mark on the World

When I stepped off the trolley with my mother, I saw Mr. Johnson breaking up his sidewalk with a sledgehammer. I started walking toward him.

"James, you get right in the house and remove your good clothes. What are you thinking of?"

I knew exactly what I was thinking of—fresh concrete—but I couldn't tell my mother that.

"Yes'm," I said.

"What do you mean, James? 'Yes' does not tell me what you are thinking."

"I mean, Yes'm, I'll go in and change my clothes. Then can I go play with Bobby?"

"May I go play."

"Yes'm. May I go play with Bobby?"

"You may, but stay within earshot. It won't be long till lunch."

I knew my secret interest in fresh concrete was safe because when my mother started a grammar lesson, her mind was clouded to everything else. For an hour Bobby and I watched Mr. Johnson breaking concrete with a sledgehammer, and we followed him as he rolled it to the woods in a wheelbarrow to fill in a gully and halt erosion.

"You boys know what I'm doing here?"

"You're hauling that concrete into the woods."

"I'm making my mark on the world. I'm trying to leave this earth a better place than I found it. It was only given to us to watch."

"What, sir?" I asked.

"The earth, boy. It was given to us to watch. And look at. We're going to bury it in trash."

Of all the things Mr. Johnson said, the thing that stuck with us was the idea of making a mark on the world. In front of Summe and Ratterman's Dairy, the city had put in a new sidewalk after a water main broke and caved in the street. The McCoy Street Gang, every last one of them, wrote their names in the wet concrete with a nail. We read them every time we went into the dairy for ice cream.

"No better than a pack of dogs pissing on bushes," my father said the first time he saw the names. I had seen dogs sniffing up and down the alley behind our house to see if any other dogs were moving into their area, and pissing to remind intruders that our alley already had enough dogs. The McCoy Street Gang carved an eye in phone poles to show where their land began, just behind Nielander's Saloon. Sometimes we walked back there and looked at the eye, but we never went past it. Hoboes did. Hoboes went everywhere.

Hoboes were men who lived down by the Licking River in camps, men who couldn't hold jobs, even during the war—men who didn't want jobs. They left messages for each other in chalk on the sidewalks the way the pioneers had blazed trails through the Kentucky woods with axe marks. We weren't allowed to mark the trees in Mr. Johnson's woods.

"You might damage the tree, son," my father said. "When Daniel Boone and Simon Kenton were wandering through here, we had a lot more trees that people. Not any more."

The hoboes' messages were in a code we couldn't crack, but one of the signs had to do with our kitchen and my mother's pies. Almost every times my mother baked, a chalk mark appeared on our corner, and a few men drifted up to our backdoor for a wedge of apple or rhubarb pie and a cup of coffee.

Then there was Kilroy, whoever he was. His name was painted on the side of the cinder block garages behind Nancy's house: "KILROY WAS HERE." He was also in the alley behind Schulte and Wisher's and in the new concrete up in front of the Greenline car barn on Madison at Twentieth. Kilroy had made his mark on the world, and we would too.

After lunch Bobby and I sat on the curb in front of my house with ten-penny nails curled in our palms, waiting.

Mr. Johnson put down a bed of gravel in the wooden forms he'd built, and tamped and leveled it. About three o'clock the Tate Builders Supply Company's huge orange and black concrete mixer groaned up the narrow street.

Mr. Johnson and the driver swung the chute into place over the waiting gravel, and viscous gray concrete slid down the chute into the form. Mr. Johnson jiggled and prodded the mass to make sure it filled all the nooks and crannies, then he and the driver ran a two-by-four across the top of the form to level the concrete.

After the truck rolled away, Mr. Johnson splashed water on the surface of the walk and began working a swirling pattern into it with a toothed trowel. By this time, Bobby and I were standing with our toes next to the form, our ten-penny nails burning holes in our palms.

"See, boys, I put a little texture in the wet concrete so it will be a little rough when it dries. That will make it better to walk on, especially when it gets wet. If you leave it smooth, it's slick as glass when it rains."

After he finished with his trowel, he sprayed the walk with a fine mist from his garden hose. Bobby and I wanted to put some texture in that sidewalk, but Mr. Johnson picked up his evening paper and sat down on a lawn chair right there by the fresh concrete. We went back to my porch to consider our situation.

We were stuck. If we were going to be immortal, have our names in concrete, be as famous as the McCoy Street Gang or Kilroy, we were going to have to employ a strategy.

When Billy came by a little later, he put the problem in a nutshell.

"Jeez, Four-eyes, we'll have to got to bed before he moves off that chair, and tomorrow that walk will be so hard we'd have to blast our names into it."

"Tonight," I said.

"Tonight, what?"

"Tonight, we'll sneak out and do it."

"When, Four-eyes?"

"Midnight."

I said my goodnights, and my mother tucked me into bed. After she left, I took my clothes out of the hamper, dressed, strapped on my six guns, and pulled on my Red Ryder gloves. I stuck the nail into my gun belt and lay back down on my bed. I was barely able to stay awake, but when the bell in the chapel tower at the hospital at the end of the street struck twelve, I opened my window and went across the porch roof and down the drain pipe to wait for Billy under the streetlight by the car tracks. I knew better that to expect Bobby. He had told me he was going to stay home.

Billy didn't come, either.

When the hospital clock struck one, I was standing under the streetlight watching the stars. Billy wasn't coming.

Whatever I was going to do to Mr. Johnson's new concrete walk, I was going to do it on my own. Billy was probably sound asleep, and I was under the street lamp watching the bats dart around the house roofs in the moonlight.

I had stayed up to see the New Year in once, but I had never been up this late in my life. On New Year's Eve I sat in my father's big leather chair in the front room and drank punch while my aunt and uncle danced, and my mother and father smiled and drank coffee and said it had been a good year, all things considered.

That was midnight and indoors. This was one o'clock outdoors, and I couldn't seem to step out of the glare of the streetlight into the strange light of the moon.

There were sounds. Night sounds. Some of them, like the ear-close buzz of a mosquito or the far-off mournful hoot of an owl, I knew. But there were other sounds. Rustlings and cracks and chunks and hisses that I had never heard before. The wind caught the gate in Nancy's yard and swung it slowly shut like the door on Inner Sanctum.

I slapped leather and went into a crouch with the six-gun in my left hand leveled toward the sound. I was reaching with my slower right hand toward the butt of the other gun when I realized I didn't even have any caps. I had nothing to protect myself from the fear and evil and death, which rode the night air as clearly as bats.

I stepped, utterly defenseless, from the ring of streetlight and walked to Mr. Johnson's fresh concrete with only a nail gripped in the cotton of my Red Ryder glove. I knelt at the corner of the walk and raised the nail, ready to drive my name deep into the concrete, deep into time.

Then I froze. I could not move. Two thoughts crossed my mind, and I was paralyzed. If I wrote my name on Mr. Johnson's walk, I would be famous and well known—especially to Mr. Johnson, who would tell my father, to whom I already felt myself to be sufficiently notorious.

The second thought was less precise, but it affected me much more. It was a memory, a memory of the day of my grandfather's funeral.

They had lowered my grandfather into a grave next to his first wife. Their names were already carved in the headstone. Her dates were complete. His birth date waited alone for the numbers that could now be worked into the stone.

My father and I walked backward in time through the graveyard as he pointed out relatives whose names were increasingly difficult to read on the weather-worn stones.

"This is your great-grandfather Huddleston. He wore himself out, wearing out land too poor to harvest rocks from. He one-cropped it to death with tobacco. It's nothing but gullies and washes now, and he's here."

I knew then I'd have my name in stone soon enough, and I knew that there were better things to do than to try to fix yourself in time by what you did. I leaned forward and pressed the thumb of my Red Ryder glove into the hardening concrete. A small mark, a thumbprint masked by the cotton of the gloves so that even Dick Tracy and the crime-stoppers couldn't lift the print from the dried concrete. My mission was complete.

I moved more lightly through the night, back to my window. I pulled at it, but it had slid shut. I couldn't raise the sash. I pried it with the barrel of my six-gun. It would not budge. I was out for the rest of the night.

I slid back down the drainpipe and sat on the porch swing, thinking, all night. I sat very still because the swing made an awful screech when it moved, and although the night was lonely, I didn't really want to see my parents just then.

I thought about a lot of things, about the differences between the street light and the moonlight and how dark it was between the stars. I thought about how the noises in the darkness scared me. I thought about a lot of things. Mr. Johnson was right. A man should leave the earth a better place. Bobby and I would spend the summer picking up trash along the street and the car tracks. It would be neat. The car tracks would be cleaner, and we would find pop bottles that were worth two cents apiece at Wiemann's Store.

By the time I had expanded the plan to include Billy and the clean-up of Garrad Street, the birds were chirping in the morning light, and my eyes were heavy. Then I heard the milkman turning the corner of the street. I scampered down the steps and around the corner of the house. Our milkman didn't miss much. He saw me duck around the corner, and as he picked up the empties next to the tin cooler box, he whispered, "I see you around there, boy. What are you doing tom-catting around at this time of the morning?"

I didn't say anything, and he put our milk into the box.

"If you're going to get up this early, you might as well come over to the dairy and help me work. At my age, I need a good tomcat to keep up my reputation." He laughed and went back to his truck.

After he left, I heard my mother open the door and take the milk in for breakfast. I waited to give her time to get back to the kitchen, then slipped up the steps and across the porch and through the door as quietly as I could. I crossed the living room and dining room and was halfway up the stairs when I heard her returning from the kitchen. I spun around on the stairs and bounded down the way I did every morning.

"Morning, Mom. What's for breakfast?"

"Oatmeal," she said, placing a tray of steaming bowls on the table. "You're up early and already dressed." Then she seemed to notice something wrong. "James, those are the same clothes you had on yesterday afternoon. You go right back upstairs and change. Hurry. This oatmeal will get cold."

"Yes'm."

Rats, Killer Turtles, and Naked Fat Men

On really hot summer days when there was nothing to do and we didn't want to do anything anyway because it was too hot, Bobby and I sat on my back steps in the shade of the big maple tree and hoped for a breeze. From where we sat I could see the place by the roots of the maple tree where my father had shot the rat.

It had happened during flood time in the spring. The Licking River went way out of its banks and drove the animals that lived along the river to higher ground. The rat, a huge slick grayish brown thing with mean red eyes and a long pink tail, had come to rest under my green wagon by the big maple tree.

I saw it as I was coming up the walk from the sandbox. I screamed and ran for the house. There was no one in the kitchen. My mother was at my Aunt Esther's that morning putting up beans. I ran up the stairs to the bathroom, where my father was shaving. I was panting and yelling.

"Rat! Rat! Rat!"

The steamy bathroom smelled of Williams Mug. My father, unperturbed by my screaming, drew his straight razor along the line of his right cheek, the lather and whiskers building up on the blade. Then he turned to me, one side of his face lathered and the other side shaved smooth, and said, "What's the matter, son?"

"Rat! There's a big rat in the backyard under my wagon by the maple tree."

My father rinsed the razor and continued to shave, running the blade down his left cheek and under his chin till his skin was smooth. "He came up from the river because of the high water," my father said. "The Licking River swarms with rats and all kinds of other fell creatures." He splashed water on his face and dried himself with a rough white towel while I watched and wondered what a fell creature was and if it could possibly be worse than the rat that was under my green wagon by the big maple tree.

"Now, son, let's go get that rat." My father went to his bedroom closet, slid his suits aside, and pulled out his bolt action single shot .22 caliber rifle.

"Reach in my shirt drawer and get some bullets."

I found the .22 cartridges in the back of the drawer next to the .32 hammerless Harrington and Richardson pocket pistol. I handed the cartridges to my father, who slid the box open and loaded the rifle.

"Open the window," he said.

"What are you going to do?" I asked as I slid the window up.

"I'm going to shoot that rat. Filthy creature."

"You'll hit my wagon."

"Don't worry, son, I know the difference between a rat and a wagon, and I come from a long line of good shots. Your great-grandfather, my granddaddy Huddleston, could light a match with a muzzle loader at thirty-five yards when he was eighty years old."

I knew that. I'd seen my great-granddaddy do that, but I didn't have too much faith in that "long line" business because I was in it too and I couldn't hit a bean can thirty-five feet away with a 4/10 shotgun. I was worried about my wagon.

My father rested the barrel of the .22 on the windowsill and waited for the rat to show himself. When that ugly little triangular head poked out, my father sighted down the barrel, exhaled slowly, and gently squeezed the trigger.

Since I was standing right beside my father and since the report echoed around the bedroom, the sound was tremendous, a quick loud crack like a water-logged branch breaking high in an old oak.

I jumped but kept my eye on the rat. The slick grayish brown triangle changed shape. The right side of the rat's head between its eye and its ear disappeared, and the rat plowed forward a few steps, clearing the wagon before it shuddered and quit moving.

"Go pick it up and throw it in the garbage," my father said as he ejected the spent cartridge.

I did not want to touch that rat. I was afraid of rats and I was afraid of dead things. I couldn't think of anything worse than touching a dead rat. I moved toward it with the same enthusiasm I had toward baths.

I picked it up by the tail. It was heavier than I had thought it would be, and it made a strange muffled thudding sound when I dropped it into the empty garbage can. I washed my hands three times a day for a week after that, and I wouldn't eat anything I had to hold with my fingers.

The good thing was that my wagon was safe. The rat was dead, and my father hadn't shot my wagon.

In fact, Bobby had his feet propped up on the wagon beside the back steps when Billy came toward us up the back walk.

"Hot enough for you, punks?"

"Sure is," said Bobby.

"I'm going over for a swim in the river. You punks want to join me?"

"I'm not allowed," said Bobby.

"Me neither," I said, and I wasn't. But it wasn't my father's stern admonition about the river that kept me away. "Son, I never want to hear that you have been anywhere near that river. It's dirty and dangerous."

True, it was dirty and dangerous. The steel company across the river in Newport blew a siren on Friday afternoon and then dumped slag right into the river. The water boiled and a cloud of steam rose up over the murky water and the dying fish. But it was the memory of the rat that kept me away from the river—that and the fact that I was a terrible swimmer.

My earliest attempts to learn to swim were in Camp Creek on my Uncle Eddie's farm in Bracken County. While my mother and father helped Eddie and Esther in a tobacco field a whistle away from the creek, I would propel myself though the shallow water with my hands grasping the muddy bottom while I kicked violently and ineffectively with my legs and kept my arms stiff to keep my chin out of the water. I called it swimming. My uncle called it bottom crawling, and he warned me not to try it anywhere else along the creek.

"You try that bottom crawling in deep water and we'll be having to pull you out like that man they had to get Porter Wells to get out of Twin Holes."

I knew that story. A group of fishermen were wading in one of the Twin Holes on Locust Creek when one of them stepped into a deep hole. His waders filled up with water, and he was so far down none of the others could reach him. Finally they had to get Porter Wells, who was the tallest man in Brooksville and who in his day had been the center of the Polar Bears basketball team, to hang onto the roots of a sycamore tree and snag that body with his feet.

There were deep holes like that all up and down both forks of Locust Creek. Camp Creek, at least the part I was swimming in, was shallow and safe except for the crawdaddies. There were lots of crawdaddies, and they all thought my fingers were lunch. They nipped at me and scared me for awhile, but I got used to them. I was determined to learn to swim, and no little crawdaddy bite was going to keep me from accomplishing my task.

Sometimes, after a day in the tobacco field, my uncle and my father would come to my swimming hole to fish for pan-sized crappies and sunfish for supper. One evening when they nearly had a fine mess of fish, my uncle hooked into a real pole bender. He worked for ten minutes before he got it to the bank, and then he wasn't sure what to do with it. It was a twenty-pound soft-shell snapping turtle.

"Never saw one that big in my life," my uncle said.

"Lucky that turtle didn't get a hold on you when you were swimming in there today, son," my father said, laughing.

"He's right about that, gimlet-butt. You wouldn't have been more than two bites for this monster. You know if he'd got hold of you he wouldn't let go till it thundered. Your bottom crawling days would have been over."

We took the turtle back to the house in a feed sack and put it in a wash tub, where I watched it claw ineffectively at the galvanized side and snap increasingly larger sticks that I offered its terrifying jaws.

At sunset my uncle turned the washtub over and struck the turtle in the head with a six-pound sledgehammer.

"Waited till sunset, gimlet-butt, because if you kill a turtle it won't die till sundown anyway."

He cut the turtle up for soup, which we had for supper the next day. I didn't have any turtle soup and I didn't ever go back swimming in Camp Creek.

My next attempt to learn to swim was at the YMCA in Covington in a pool that was so clean and clear that you could see the bottom and see that there were no creatures lurking in the murk to take bites out of you.

"We pride ourselves on the cleanliness of our pool," Mr. Delbert, the instructor, said. "We want you to take pride in it too, and we want you to help us keep it clean. You will take a shower and go through the footbath on the way to the pool, and you will never wear a bathing suit in the pool. Suits give off lint and put a strain on our filter. We don't want that. Now get undressed and meet me on the pool deck after your showers."

As much as I wanted to learn to swim, I didn't think much of the notion of standing around naked with a bunch of other boys. I didn't know what to do with my hands, and I wondered if the girls' swimming classes had similar rules. That would be something to see.

"I see some of you boys have your little periscopes raised. The cold water will take care of that. Get into the pool—shallow end. Now put your face in the water."

The lessons proceeded week after week. Mr. Delbert was a good instructor, and we learned the dead man's float, the dog paddle, the American crawl, the backstroke, and the breaststroke. Back and forth across the shallow end of the pool we went, honing our skills, getting ready for the test we knew would come.

"Next week you are going to have a test. You can use any stroke you have learned to swim the length of the pool, from the deep end down there by the diving boards, all the way up here to the wall on the shallow end. Remember your glide stroke. You can use your glide stroke to rest if you get tired."

The next week I chose the American crawl, and I got tired and remembered the glide stroke. I kicked out into my glide. I thought I was resting. Mr. Delbert thought I was drowning. He said I was gliding under water. Anyway, he jumped in next to me, and his big hairy arm hit my side. Mr. Delbert was a big man, and the impact of his arm took the air right out of me while his naked bulk took us both to the bottom. He quickly twisted me into a cross-chest carry and pushed off the bottom of the pool into a steady sidestroke. When we reached the side of the pool, I puked up a little water, and he flunked me on my swimming test.

After that I didn't really try anymore. I figured it wouldn't matter much that I was a weak swimmer. My parents weren't about to join a country club, and in Kentucky there isn't a lot of beachfront property. Our family never argued about whether we should go to the mountains or the seashore because my Uncle Bill lived in the mountains. We went there every summer like a clock.

I was just as glad that I was a poor swimmer because that way I wasn't tempted to go near that river.

But it was hot. Bobby seemed to read my mind.

"Maybe your mother would let us turn on your garden hose."

"I'll ask her," I said, and I twisted around on the steps to yell through the screen door into the kitchen. "Mother, can Bobby and me turn on the hose?"

"James, when will you ever learn?" asked my mother, coming to the backdoor with a half-shucked roasting ear in her hand.

"It's 'May Bobby and I turn on the hose.'"

"Yes'm. May we?"

"You may."

We did, and the water was so cool and slick moving over my body that I knew then that in spite of rats, killer turtles, and naked fat men, I would have to learn to swim someday.

Four-eyes and the Midgets

Of course I knew better. Billy was always getting me into trouble—like the time he dared me to steal a pickle out of the jar on the bar down at Nielander's Saloon—but there was something in his voice when he said it that made me fall for it even though I could hear my mother saying, "James, one of these days Master North is going to tell you to jump off the Suspension Bridge, and you're going to do it." I stood there looking down the alley toward the corner where the midget's house was. Then I turned back toward Billy and Bobby.

"You ain't goin' to do it, are you, Four-eyes?"

"Of course he ain't goin' to, Bobby-baby. You know ol' Four-eyes here is chicken."

"I'll do it."

"All the way up to the attic window in the front?"

"Yep."

"Oh, come on Four-eyes. You can't do that. Don't you remember what Ralph told us about them havin' a regular-sized brother and all?"

"Yep. I remember."

"Well?"

"Well, I just can't go on lettin' Billy call me a chicken all the time. I ain't no chicken."

"Okay, Four-eyes. You ain't no chicken. I won't call you a chicken anymore. Okay?"

"Okay, what?"

"We'll just forget the whole thing, okay?"

"Nope. I said I'd do it, and I'm gonna do it."

"When?"

"Right now. They always go shopping before supper. You two can stand across the street and yell if you see them turn the corner down at Nielander's."

We walked the block to the end of the alley together. When we reached the hedge by the corner, Billy and Bobby crossed the street, and I slipped through the hedge and started for the house. That wasn't hard. We'd done that before. Billy first, then me, and finally Bobby. We'd cut through the hedge run across the yard, beat on the door, then run like hell before one of them could open the door and catch us. Then there was the mailbox.

Ralph said once some of the McCoy Street Gang lit a sack of shit on the midgets' porch on Cabbage Night and one of the brothers got it all over his feet trying to put out the fire. Billy said that we ought to try that sometime. Billy said a lot of things. Like he said that I was too chicken to go inside the midgets' house and wave to him out of the attic window.

I stood for a moment in the living room with my hand still on the door while my eyes adjusted to the change in light. The heavy drapes were drawn, and the room was dark. It was a strange room—filled with old heavy furniture like my grandmother's—and there were bundles of old newspapers and magazines everywhere. I pushed the door behind me and crossed the room to the stairs. They, too, were cluttered with magazines and newspapers tied in small bundles and stacked so that only a narrow passage was clear on the steps. I wound my way up two flights to the second floor, then up a long straight flight to the attic.

The clutter was worse in the attic than on the stairs. There were several dressmaker's dummies, a number of large old trunks, a baby carriage, and more magazines and newspapers. I could not find a light switch, so I made my way across the littered floor by the light from the distant, soot-covered window. I tripped twice—once knocking over an old birdcage.

Finally I made it to the window and began to rub the grime off to see out.

When I could finally see, there was no one to see, no one to wave to. Bobby and Billy were gone.

The thumping sound could have been my heart, but it was too far off. It seemed to be coming from the other end of the attic from the stairwell opening. It sounded like someone coming up the stairs.

Since I'd wiped the soot off, the light from the window was stronger now. As he turned toward me out of the stairwell, he squinted against the brightness. I moved closer to the wall so that I would be out of the light and took a few tentative steps toward the stairwell. Then I tripped on the birdcage. He turned toward the sound. I ducked behind a trunk.

"Come on out. I know you're up here."

I leaped from behind the trunk and pushed the dressmaker's dummy toward him. It bowled him over, and he started screaming as I turned toward the stairs. There was no time to thread my way through the stacks of magazines. I rolled and slid and fell, knocking the stacks every which way.

I landed on the second floor on my back with my feet up the stairway. I was looking up at a small man with a very large pistol.

"I got him, Rudy. Come on down."

I could hear the other one still screaming and thrashing around up in the attic. I started to roll over. The one with the gun spoke to me.

"Don't move."

I didn't. I just lay there thinking about what Ralph had said about their other brother and that restaurant in Cincinnati, while the one I'd knocked down pushed his way through the tangle of papers on the stairs. Finally I could see him standing on a clear space on the step just above my feet.

"For Christ's sake, Jules, put that thing away. You might hurt somebody."

"He's a thief. We've caught him red-handed. We've got rights just like anyone else."

"Jules. The gun."

"Oh, all right. But I think we ought to make an example of this one."

"Jules."

The one holding the gun frowned, then lowered the gun, and disappeared from my field of vision.

"You're one of the young people from up the alley, aren't you?"

"Yes, sir."

"Get up, young man."

"Yes, sir. Thank you, sir."

I did, and for the first time, I became aware of his size. Standing above me on the stairs, especially with his brother standing over me with a gun, he had looked big. Now I could see that he was about my size. His head was huge, his arms and legs short.

"Downstairs." He pointed.

"Yes, sir." I picked my way through the magazines and newspapers down the half flight of stairs to the landing. When I turned to go down the final half flight, I stared into the upturned faces of the other two, the brother who had held the gun and the sister. The one with me spoke.

"Molly, we will have some tea. Our young friend here will have a glass of milk. Is there any of that Dutch apple pie left?"

She didn't say anything, but she turned and threaded her way through the magazines toward the back of the house. The one with me pointed, and I followed. In the kitchen he pointed again at a chair, and I sat. She was cutting the pie. The other one sat on the counter with his feet hanging in the air.

"Why did you come in here, young man?"

"You know why, Rudy. You know why. Because he's mean. They're all mean. Remember those kids that blew up our mailbox?"

"Now Jules, calm down. Let him tell it. Why, young man?"

"Billy said that I was chicken, and I said that I wasn't. Please, mister, don't kill me. I know that is how you make money, but don't kill me. My daddy would pay money to get me back. Please don't kill me. Please."

"Kill you? What are you talking about?"

I couldn't answer. I was too frightened, and I sat there sobbing for a long time. Finally I couldn't cry anymore, but I had the hiccups.

"Here, drink this."

I took the water and drank it slowly. The hiccups subsided, and I handed the empty glass back to the one seated across from me.

"Now tell me what it is you think we do."

"Ralph. He lives across the street from me. Ralph says you've got a regular-sized brother in Cincinnati who runs a restaurant and that he pays cash money for ground-up kids to make soup out of."

The one on the kitchen counter let out a high funny cackle till the other one motioned toward him with his stubby hand and he stopped. Just then the kettle screamed. The sister poured the water into the teapot and then set four slices of pie on the table. Then she and the one on the kitchen counter sat down at the table while the one called Rudy poured the tea.

"Oh, his milk. I forgot his milk," she said jumping up. She poured it, placed it in front of me, and sat back down.

"Do you believe the story?"

I took a bite of pie and a short swallow of milk while I thought that one over.

"No, sir. I don't."

"That's good because it's not true, and we ought to know, right, Jules?"

"That's right, Rudy."

"You see, young man, we know that the story is not true because we made the story up ourselves."

"You made the story up?" I looked puzzled.

"That's right. Years ago, when we first came into this neighborhood."

"Why?"

"Because you're all alike. That's why. Because you're..."

"That's enough, Jules. Young man, as you grow up, you will discover that there is great pressure in society to make everyone alike. We can't be like everyone. We are different. It is very difficult to be different. It is easier to be alone."

"So you made up the story to keep everyone away."

"Yes. That one and a number of others that you will run into as you grow older."

"Would you like another slice of pie?"

"Yes'm. I would."

She got the pie, and when she set it in front of me, she spoke to the one called Rudy.

"They're up the alley by the Green's garage, the other ones."

"She means your friends. One of them, I assume, is Billy, the one who put you up to this."

"Yes, sir."

"They mustn't find out, Rudy. We can't let them find out. It will be awful again like it was at first."

"Jules," he said, holding his stubby hand palm out toward his brother. Then he turned toward me. "You must promise not to tell them. Not to tell anyone."

"Yes, sir."

"And one more thing."

"Yes'm. What's that?"

"Would you promise to come back sometime alone to talk to us? You could have more pie."

"Yes'm. I'd like that."

"Fine, young man. Now here's the plan."

The plan was really neat. The three midgets stood in the middle of the kitchen and stomped and screamed and beat on pots while I shot out the backdoor, ran across the yard, and darted through the hedge.

"Jeez, Four-eyes, what happened? We heard all this screaming. Then it got quiet."

"Real quiet."

"Yeah. Then there was this awful racket and you come runnin' out the back."

"I thought you was a goner, Four-eyes. For sure. I thought you was done for."

"Me, too. What happened in there, Four-eyes?"

"Well, Bobby, I'll tell you. It's goin' to take more than three midgets to make soup out of me."

"Jeez, Four-eyes. You mean it's true what Ralph said?"

"I reckon it is, Billy. They even have a big butcher's block and one of those cleavers right in the middle of the kitchen."

"Boy. I ain't gonna mess with them midgets again ever. What about you, Four-eyes?"

"Me neither," I said with the fingers of my left hand crossed behind my back as I walked slowly up the alley toward my backyard.

The Kiss

One Saturday in August, a big yellow moving truck rolled up to a house down the street, and Phyllis and Elaine moved away and left my next door neighbor, Nancy, with no one to play with. They were the only other girls on the block, and they were Nancy's best friends. It was tough on her.

"I miss Phyllis and Elaine," she said. "Now I don't have anyone to play dolls with."

It was tough on me, too. Phyllis and Elaine were both slow, and I could always count on being able to tag one or the other of them in a game of catchers. Nancy, on the other hand, was lean and quick and could outrun any of us over a short distance. Billy could run farther, but no one could run faster.

"I miss them too," I said. "Remember the time Phyllis let that whole jar of lightning bugs loose in their room because she thought they looked like stars?"

"Her mom was so mad."

"Yeh."

"Four-eyes, you want to play some dolls? I'll let you play with my mother's china doll."

"I don't want to play dolls."

"Please. I don't have anyone to play with anymore."

"Dolls are girl stuff. I'm going to the woods and play some baseball."

"Can I play?"

"I don't know. We'll have to ask Billy and Bobby."

I didn't know how Billy and Bobby would react to Nancy wanting to play baseball with us in the woods. We played almost every day in the summer when we weren't playing cowboys and badmen or big game hunting. Nancy played cowboys with us sometimes because she could be Dale Evans, Queen of the West. That made sense. But a girl playing baseball?

Billy and Bobby and I collected baseball cards. I had most of the Reds. Billy was a Cardinals fan. He liked the way they got into bench-clearing brawls.

"The Cards might lose a lot of games," he said proudly, "but they never lose a fight."

Bobby, who had five different gloves including a catcher's mitt and a first baseman's mitt, as well as eleven bats, a chest protector, a catcher's mask, and shin guards, was a Yankees fan.

We followed our teams on the sports pages of the local papers. Bobby's father read the morning *Enquirer* before he left for work in Cincinnati. Billy's dad liked the afternoon *Post* because it had the best information on horse racing. My father took the afternoon *Times-Star* because he liked the paper's stand against the gangsters who hung out in Newport.

No matter which paper I read, the news from Crosley Field was sad. The Reds were terrible. I loved them anyway, and at meals, or during enforced rests visited upon me by my mother, who was convinced I was going to run myself ragged, or at night, I would listen to Waite Hoyt broadcasting home games from Crosley Field or reconstructing the road games from a teletype wire in the studio.

We knew the batting averages of all the Reds players, and we even knew who might be brought up from the farm teams for a late season look. We knew baseball, but none of us had ever been to a game. Bobby's father was always too busy to take him. Billy's father was either drunk or at the racetrack. My father—well, my father just didn't seem to me to be the type who went to the ballpark. So I was really shocked at breakfast one Saturday morning when he said, "Son, I want you to get to bed early tonight. I have two tickets to tomorrow's doubleheader with Boston, and you and I are going to the ballgame."

I didn't say anything. I just sat there. I couldn't believe it.

"Well, son," my mother said, "what do you have to say?"

"Neat. I mean thank you. Can I be excused? I have to go to the woods and tell Billy and Bobby."

"Finish drinking your milk first."

"Yes'm." I downed my milk in nothing flat.

"James."

"Yes'm."

"Wipe that milk moustache off your lip."

"Yes'm." I did and said, "Excuse me," and was out the front door before my father finished saying, "You're excused."

Later that night, as I was lying in bed wondering what it would be like to actually step up to the plate against a big league pitcher and have him throw a fastball right across the heart of the plate, I realized that we would have to miss church to get to the game on time. That didn't really bother me; in fact, that made going to the ballgame even better. I was always trying to figure out ways to miss church. Sunday school was all right. In fact I liked Sunday school. I had a pin for being in Sunday school every Sunday for a whole year.

In Sunday school you got to do stuff. Once I made a little reed boat like the one Moses was found in; it even floated. But in church after the second hymn you just sat back and took it from the minister until after the offering. It was worse than school. At least in school the teacher asked you questions or had you read. In church you just had to sit there, and my legs always went to sleep during the sermon.

I sort of wanted to go to Sunday school because if I could get through another year without missing, I would get a bar to hang from my attendance pin that would say "Two Years."

My father had a little blue and gold "20" under his Kiwanis pin, which meant that he had attended a Kiwanis meeting once every week for twenty years. He worked hard at that.

Sometimes when we were on vacations, mother and I would wind up eating lunch in a diner in some town we'd never seen before while my father went off to have lunch with a bunch of Kiwanians he had never seen before and would never see again. That way he didn't miss his meeting. Twenty years—and I was just working on my second one.

The next day I kept my string alive. We all went to Sunday School, and then my father and I drove across the Suspension Bridge to Cincinnati. My mother attended church, went home up Madison Avenue on the #6 Rosedale street car, and listened to Waite Hoyt broadcast the ballgame on the radio.

We paid $2.00 to park our big green four-door Hudson in a vacant lot several blocks from the ball park in a neighborhood that, even at 11:30 a.m. on a bright and sunny morning, made me glad my father was walking right beside me.

"Watch your car for fifty cents," a young black man said to my father as we walked out of the lot.

My father ignored him.

"Why did he say that?" I asked. "Why did he say he would watch our car for fifty cents?"

"Because he's practicing to be a criminal," said my father. "He's trying to extort money from me. They're absolutely everywhere. The *Times-Star* is right. The criminal element is taking over society. We must stand up to them. We must never give an inch."

I was sorry I'd asked the question. Whenever my father got started on criminals or gamblers, he could go on for hours.

"They even tried to take over baseball once, son. Only time the Reds ever won the World Series was when the gamblers had bought the other team, the Chicago White Sox. But Judge Landis took care of them."

I didn't know the Reds had ever won the World Series. I didn't know they'd ever finished in the first division. I thought they'd always been trying to fight their way out of, or trying to avoid falling into, the National League cellar. But that didn't matter.

We covered maybe three blocks, crossed a wide street, and finally stood on the sidewalk crowded with vendors outside the big green walls of Crosley Field.

There were men selling everything: peanuts, pennants, popcorn, soft drinks. The newsmen were crying the disasters of the day. It was September 18, 1949, and things were happening all over the world.

207 People Lose Their Lives
As Cruise Ship Noronic Burns

North Atlantic Treaty Council
Outlines Mutual Defense Plans

Jewish Leader: Israel/
Jerusalem Indissoluble

French Send More Troops
To Stabilize Viet Nam

We passed all the vendors, handed our tickets to an usher who tore then in two and gave my father the rain checks, pushed through the turnstile, bought a scorecard, and headed for our seats.

Our seats were back of first base and the home team dugout, far enough up in the lower deck to be under the shade of the upper deck. The sun was bright on the manicured grass of the infield. Sitting there in my blue Sunday suit, looking straight out over the leftfield wall toward the laundry across the street which sported the placard "Hit this sign and win a free suit," I was glad for the shade and glad for the breeze that seemed to blow from behind us straight out toward centerfield, where the flag on the scoreboard rode like a wind sock directing flyballs to homerville.

On September 18, 1949, my world was a bright green ball field stretched out in front of me and a double header between the Cincinnati Reds and the Boston Braves.

The Reds at 57 and 84 were in seventh place, 33 games behind the league leading the St. Louis Cardinals. Boston was stuck in fourth place, 21 back, but only a game and a half in front of the fifth place New York Giants. The real battle in the National League was between St. Louis and the Brooklyn Dodgers, who were only 2 games back. The sound of that battle was far away from the din in Crosley Field.

The noise in Crosley Field was mostly caused by the vendors.

"Beer here. Get your ice cold Hudepohl Beer."

"Red Hots. Get your Red Hots."

"Do you want a hot dog, son?"

"No, sir."

"Lemonade. Ice cold lemonade."

"Peanuts. Peanuts. Peanuts."

"How about some peanuts and lemonade? Would you like them?"

"Yes, sir."

My father signaled the vendors, and we passed a five-dollar bill down the row of spectators to the aisle. The vendors sent a bag of peanuts, a lemonade, and the correct change back up the aisle and went on.

"Peanuts. Peanuts. Peanuts."

"Lemonade. Ice cold lemonade."

The peanuts and lemonade were good, and the Reds scored four runs in the bottom of the first behind the pitching of Johnny Vander Meer. The Braves scored one in the third and one in the fifth before a four-run outburst in the top of the seventh. Ewell Blackwell relieved Vander Meer and shut the Braves down for two innings while the Reds clawed their way back to a tie with a run in the seventh and another one in the eighth. Fox relieved Blackwell in the ninth and got the win when Virgil Stallcup singled scoring Ted Kluszewski from second base.

The second game was a pitcher's duel between Cincinnati rookie Harry Perkowski and the Braves journeyman Johnny Sain. It ended in a 1-1 tie after 9 innings and was played off the next day, an open date for both clubs. The Braves won 6-2.

That Monday, while the Braves were beating the Reds, I was busy losing my best friends over a baseball.

In the bottom of the sixth inning of the first game the Cincinnati centerfielder Lloyd Merriman fouled a pitch a mile high back of first base.

"If someone doesn't catch that, it will bounce," my father said.

No one caught it, and it did bounce off the metal superstructure of the first base box seats in a high arc to my father's hand. Without getting up, my father, in his three-piece suit with his hat on, reached up and snagged the sphere from the air. He handed it to me, and I put it in my pocket and watched the game.

"It's his first game," I heard my father say.

"What luck," someone near us said. "I've been coming all my life and I've never caught a ball."

When we got home I wanted to trick my mother. I hid the ball in my coat so it rolled off the table when she picked my coat up to put it away.

"Look!" I shouted. "Daddy caught a foul ball."

"I thought maybe he had," my mother said. "Waite Hoyt said on the radio that a man in a suit, wearing a hat, grabbed a foul with one hand without even getting up and handed it to a boy in a suit next to him."

"And with 5,926 fans in Crosley Field, you knew from that description that I had caught a foul ball?" said my father.

My mother ignored him for a moment, straightened her apron, and then said, "How many folks did you see at the ballgame wearing three-piece suits and hats?"

"How was the ballgame?" Billy asked the next day as soon as I got to the woods with my ball glove.

"It was really neat. My father caught a foul ball."

"He didn't," said Billy.

"I don't believe it," said Bobby.

"He did," said Nancy, "I saw it on the mantel in Four-eyes living room."

"Show me," said Billy.

"Let's play ball with it," said Bobby.

"No," I said. "I'm not allowed."

"Whose ball is it? Didn't your father give it to you?"

"Yeh, he gave it to me, but I'm not allowed to play with it. It's a souvenir. Anyway, we've got lots of balls. How many balls do we need to play a game here in the woods?"

"We don't have any real, honest to God, genuine big league balls," said Billy.

"Yeh, Four-eyes. That's a real-life major league ball," said Bobby. "We could play with it."

"No," I said.

"Four-eyes, I'll let you have my second best jack knife if you let us play with that ball."

"No, Billy."

"I'll let you have my first baseman's glove."

"To keep?"

"Yes, to keep."

"It's a right-handed, Bobby. What would I do with a right-handed glove?"

"If you let us play with your ball, I'll give you a kiss," said Nancy.

"A kiss?" said Billy.

"A kiss?" said Bobby.

"A kiss," I said. "That's stupid, Nancy. Big league ball players are like cowboys. They don't have time for girls and that kind of mushy stuff."

"Come on," said Billy. "I know what we can do. We can go put pennies on the car tracks."

"What will happen?" Bobby said.

"It mashes 'em flat."

"Can I go too?" asked Nancy.

"No!" the three of us said in unison.

Gangbusters

I was sitting in the corner of the sandbox peeling the bark off a twig when Billy came striding down the alley past the garage and leaned on the back gate.

"Watcha up to, Four-eyes?"

"Nuthin'."

"Where's Bobby-baby?"

"Newport. His old aunt's sick. He had to go over and see her."

"Newport! Wow! Some punks have all the luck. He'll probably see gangsters all over the place."

"Gangsters?"

"Sure, punk," said Billy as he opened the back gate. He crouched, pointed his index finger, and covered the yard with his empty hand. He moved toward me still in a crouch, dived into a forward roll, and landed prone on his stomach with his empty right-handed index finger pointed, braced on his left, level on me.

"Ka-pow. Ka-pow. Gotcha, Four-eyes." Billy leaped to his feet and stood over me.

I jerked twice as the slugs tore through my body then pitched slowly forward into the cold sand.

"You really die good, Four-eyes—better than Bobby."

I rolled over and smiled up through the fringe of the maple tree and the tattered chasing clouds. It was better than getting the Academy Award.

"Are there really gangsters in Newport, Billy?"

"Sure, punk. Lots of 'em. Here too. But not so many."

I sat up fast and looked at Billy. "Here?" I breathed. "Gangsters here?"

"Sure, punk. They drive big, black cars and they're always in Whitey's Barber Shop up on Madison."

Whitey's was where Dad took me. It was near the corner of Twentieth and Madison. There were seven chairs in Whitey's, but Whitey was the only barber, and we always had to wait for our haircuts. I didn't mind because Whitey always had the latest comic books, and I was allowed to read them in the barber shop.

"I never saw any."

"Of course not, punk. They're in the backroom."

Backroom. There was a backroom—at least there was a doorway covered by a heavy pink drape.

"My old man says Whitey's runnin' a horse parlor in his backroom."

I didn't ask Billy what a horse parlor was. I just nodded and said, "horse parlor" in a tone that was meant to show that I'd heard it all before.

"Why don't we go up there and have a look, Billy?"

"Sure, punk, then we can go for a dip in the river in our concrete swimming trunks. Those boys ain't like the make-believe bad men you and Bobby-baby chase through the woods. You mess with them and they sell you to the midgets to make soup out of."

I picked up a shovel and began to fill a rusty pail with sand. Billy sat down on the edge of the sandbox and started smoothing the sand with his palm, then stood up and spit into the sand.

"Hell, Four-eyes, let's go."

The streetlights came on as we turned the corner of Twentieth and Madison. Whitey's was empty. Whitey sat in the first chair reading the *Times-Star* surrounded by the vari-colored litter of his day's work. The shop smelled of wintergreen and pomade.

"Hi, boys," said Whitey, looking over the top of the sports page. "Haircut?"

"No, sir," I hesitated. "Could I use your bathroom?"

"Sure, son. It's there in the back on the left through that pink curtain."

Billy and I walked slowly through the shop toward the pink curtain. As we passed each of the six empty chairs Billy dipped, grabbed the footrest, and gave the chair a spin. We covered the last few feet and I pulled the drape back. Nothing. No horse parlor, no gangsters. Just a small dark hallway with the bathroom door on the left and the heavy outside door in front of us. I reached out and pulled open the big door.

Whitey's was larger than I had ever imagined. The door opened into a brightly-lighted room as big as the shop out front. Seven men sat at a long table at the left talking into telephones and writing on small pads. Above them on a raised catwalk, two men moved about, writing numbers on the blackboard that covered the whole left wall. A speaker above us over the door droned, "They are running the third at Santa Anita..."

"Wow, Four-eyes."

When Billy spoke, a tall man in a dark blue suit, who had been standing in the middle of the room watching the numbers go up on the wall, turned toward us.

"Do something for you, boys?"

"My friend, James, here needs to go to the bathroom. Mr. Whitey sent us back here."

Something seemed to flicker in the man's eye, then it was gone. He raised his empty right hand, pointed his index finger, and leveled it at us.

"It's right through the door on the right. You can't..." He broke off when one of the men from the table yelled that the connection to Miami was gone. That flicker came back into his eyes.

"Goddamn phone company. How the hell is a guy supposed to run a business when all he gets is shit for service?"

We closed the door, passed through the pink curtain, and walked the length of the shop.

"Find it all right?" Whitey asked without looking up from the paper.

"Yes, sir. Thank you."

Outside Billy started running, then stopped and waited by the drugstore until I came up to him.

"Come on, Four-eyes. We've seen the operation. They'll be after us. We got to move."

"Those guys aren't gangsters, Billy," I said, looking down at the dull pavement.

Billy pranced beside me, still ready to dash at the first sign of a long black car.

"Not gangsters? What do you mean? That tall guy looked just like that Legs Diamond we saw at the Shirley last week."

"I don't now what his name is, but that tall guy sings in the choir at my church every Sunday."

We walked slowly down Twentieth street with our hands in our pockets. It was dark as we turned the corner onto Garrad Street. We could see the lights twinkling among the grapevines on the patio at Nielander's Saloon.

Finally Billy said, "Hell, punk, let's go see if Bobby-baby's back from Newport. Maybe he saw some real gangsters."

Hands Up, We've Got You Covered

Bobby and Nancy and I were sitting in the shade of the big oak trees at the edge of the woods, looking down on the car tracks, when Billy came around the corner, kicking a can. Billy was getting older. He ran around a lot with the McCoy Street Gang. We seldom saw him anymore except at night. He'd come by, when we were chasing fireflies, and talk to Nancy under the street light at the end of Maryland Avenue. Nancy used to be the best lightning bug catcher on the block, but that summer she'd just talk and talk with Billy under the streetlight.

"Hi, punks. What ya up to?" Billy always talked like that. His hero was Humphrey Bogart, and only the day's oppressive heat kept him from wearing his trench coat.

"Nothing. We were playing flies and grounders, but it's too hot."

"Too hot for flies and grounders, eh Four-eyes? How about some cowboys and badmen?"

"Great. I'll be the Lone Ranger and Bobby can be Tonto."

"Nix, Four-eyes. We need some badmen. You and Bobby can be the Dalton boys. I'll be Red Ryder, and Nancy here can be my Little Beaver."

"Don't talk like that, Billy. They don't know a thing about that," snapped Nancy.

Boy, girls are dumb sometimes. Red Ryder was on the radio every Monday night, and Dad said when I got to be twelve he'd get me a Daisy Red Ryder B-B Gun.

"Well, what they don't know won't hurt 'em, eh, Little Beaver?"

"What's he talking about, Nancy?"

"Never mind, Bobby. You and Four-eyes get your guns and get saddled up and attack us. We'll be in the clubhouse. That'll be our ranch house."

"Why don't you be Dale Evans, and Billy could be Roy Rogers, King of the Cowboys?"

"OK Four-eyes. I'll be Roy and..."

"They're married."

"So?"

"Billy's got a girlfriend. Billy's got a girlfriend. Billy's got a g..."

"Listen, punk," growled Billy, moving toward me with his fist clenched. "Do you want to play or not?"

"Sure, Billy."

"OK then, vamoose. Give us to five hundred by ones, then try to sneak up on us."

Bobby and I rode off on Blacky and Flash. We rode down the car tracks to the corner of Wiemann's Grocery, counting all the way.

"97, 98, 99, 100, 101..."

We rode down Eastern Avenue and up Twenty-first Street past the hospital.

"274, 275, 276, 277..."

We rode by the midgets' house over to Garrad Street and past Nielander's Saloon.

"399, 400, 401, 402, 403..."

Then we turned back to the car tracks and headed for the woods.

"496, 497, 498, 499, 500."

"I'll follow the ditch to the middle of the woods. You go around through your yard and come up on them from behind."

"OK Four-eyes. How will I know when to open fire?"

"Hold your fire. We'll get as close as we can. Maybe we can take them as hostages."

"Neat. Giddup, Blacky."

I tied Flash to one of the oak trees and started to crawl up the ditch toward the clubhouse. Every few feet I stopped to listen. I couldn't hear a thing, and I thought maybe they'd tricked us and were waiting in ambush somewhere. Then I heard Nancy giggle. I could see Bobby crawling out of the flowerbed at the back of his house. I gave him the secret hand signal that meant, "advance quietly." He joined me under the window of the clubhouse just as Nancy giggled again. We drew our guns and leaped up, leveling them through the window.

"Hands up. We've got you cov..."

Nancy screamed, pushed Billy away from her, and rolled away from the window, buttoning her shirt. Billy just sat there with a silly grin on his face.

Finally he stood up with his hands up and took a few rolling steps forward. When he finally spoke, he didn't sound like Bogart at all. He sounded like that big John Wayne guy Bobby and I saw in *Red Sky* at the Shirley.

"Well, Four-eyes, I guess you caught us this time."

The Gun

It was summer. It was always summer when I was growing up, and I was always playing in the cool, shady, two-block-long abandoned street car right-of-way that ran between Eastern Avenue and Garrad Street. My street, Maryland Avenue, ran dead into the car tracks, and I could cover the distance from my porch to the fireplug where the gang always met, before the screen door slammed.

It was summer, and Billy North and I were goofing around by the car tracks. Billy was slashing through the piles of leaves that lay rotting where Mr. Johnson had dumped them the year before or the year before that. Suddenly, Billy whistled and quickly picked something up. A gun. It was a small, black handled revolver with a badly rusted barrel.

"A gun," we both breathed together.

"How do you 'spose it got there?"

"The killer dropped it on his getaway, stupid," Billy said.

"Let me see it."

"Sure, kid." Billy leveled the rusty barrel right at my eyes.

"Geez, Billy, that's a real gun."

"You're such a chicken, Four-Eyes. Look, it's not even loaded." Billy snapped the revolver and exposed the empty chamber.

"Maybe we should call the police."

"Why?" said Billy as he spun and clicked the empty revolver at a band of pirates who were just ducking behind Mr. Neal's garage.

"So they could catch the killers."

"Bang! Bang!... It was probably Mr. Johnson or Dickie Wiemann. Anyway, if you tell, you'll be a tattletale."

"Maybe it was the midgets."

"Boy, if you tell on them, they'll grind you up for soup."

"I think we'd better tell."

"Look, kid, I'm going to keep this gun. Finder keepers, losers weepers. And if you tell, I'll kill you."

Billy looked at me, stuck the gun in the waistband of his blue jeans, and headed toward his house on Garrad Street. I stood there in the cool shade of the car tracks until he went up the steps to his house.

The next day Billy had the gun in the waistband of his shorts when I met him out by the car tracks.

"I see you got the gun, Billy."

"Yeh, punk, I've got the gun, but I don't have any bullets. Gun is no good without bullets."

"Bullets?"

"Yeh. If we had some bullets, we could go into the woods and shoot at targets."

"My dad has bullets."

"Where?"

"In his bureau drawer under his shirts; he keeps them there."

"Get 'em."

"What?"

"Go get some bullets and we'll try this sucker out."

"I don't know, Billy."

"I don't know, Billy! You're beginning to sound like Bobby-baby. Are you chicken, Four-eyes?"

"I ain't chicken, but my father told me never to mess with his gun."

"Gun? He has a gun?"

"Of course he has a gun. What do you think the bullets are for?"

"Get it. Get it and get the bullets. We can really have some fun."

I did it almost without thinking. I went into my parents' bedroom, opened the top drawer in my father's bureau, and took the hammerless .32 caliber revolver from the leather holster under the shirts. Then I reached into the far back corner and took the box of shells. I slid them into my jacket pocket, slipped out of the bedroom, and headed back to the car tracks.

Billy was impressed.

"Geez, Four-eyes, that's a neat gun."

It wasn't a very neat gun at all. It was old and dirty and heavy. The grip had a deep-cut crisscross scoring that hurt your hand when you held it.

"Let me see it, Four-eyes."

I handed the revolver to Billy. "Be careful. There's no safety on it."

"I never saw a gun like this. There's no hammer. You can't tell when it's going to fire. What kind is it?"

"It's a Harrington and Richardson."

"Never heard of a Harrington and Richardson."

Billy handed the gun back to me butt first, holding it with his finger on the trigger guard and letting the gun roll forward.

"Give me some bullets and I'll load up, then we can have some real fun."

I handed Billy five shells. He pulled his pistol from his belt, broke it open against the back of his knee, and tried to insert the cartridges.

"Shit."

"What's wrong?"

"These bullets won't fit; they're too big."

"They're .32's."

"Well, this must be a .22 or something. Shit. Now we'll both have to use your gun. We'll take turns, okay?"

"Okay."

Billy jammed the .22 back into the waistband of his shorts and held his hand out for my father's revolver.

"What are we going to aim at?"

"Till we get used to the action of this gun, we'll aim at the shed."

"Mr. Johnson's shed?"

"How many sheds do you see out here, Four-eyes?"

Billy held the gun at his side like a cowboy ready to draw from a holster. Then his hand moved like a snake, and there was a deafening roar long before Billy's hand and the gun were level with the shed.

The smell of cordite hung in the air. Three feet in front of us there was a neat hole where the .32 slug had entered the soft earth.

"Damn, Four-eyes. You can't tell when this damn thing is going to go off. I could have blown my foot off."

"My turn."

"Your turn? I didn't even get to aim."

"Doesn't matter. You shot. We're taking turns. It's my turn."

Billy reluctantly handed me the gun. I leveled it on a new board in the center of the shed, holding it steady with both hands.

"Who the hell do you think you are, Four-eyes, Ned Buntline?"

I didn't answer. I let my breath out slowly and slowly squeezed the trigger. The sound came out before I expected it to, and the roar was followed by a scream.

Before I smelled the cordite, I saw Billy heading down the bank toward the car tracks. I knew it was time to move.

I had reloaded the gun and the remaining bullets back in my father's shirt drawer before the ambulance pulled away from the curb in front of Mr. Johnson's house.

"I never heard of anything like it in my life," my father said with a forkful of mashed potatoes halfway to his mouth.

“Well, that’s what happened. The bullet came right through the second story bedroom wall and hit him in the leg. He was in bed fast asleep because he’s on night shift this week. He was able to get to the phone and call the hospital. Son, do you want some more beans?”

“No’m.” I didn’t want any more anything, especially any more discussion of the strange shooting incident that had occurred at the house across the street. My mother’s roast beef was usually a little tough and dry and got larger as you chewed it. The piece I had in my mouth had grown by about 35 percent by the time my father said, “Do they know who did it?”

“No. The police were up and down the street all afternoon, asking questions. Nobody saw or heard anything. The police didn’t find a thing.”

The roast beef had doubled in volume and was sucking all the moisture out of my body.

“Likely they never will,” my father said. “If they’re too dumb to see a slot machine in a candy store, they’ll never find a man who shot someone asleep in his bed. I have a meeting at the church tonight to discuss the ineptitude of our city’s finest. I guess I’d better go upstairs and put on a fresh shirt. What are you doing tonight, son?”

I don’t know which was worse, the thought of my father opening that drawer and smelling cordite, or the knowledge that my uncle was right: I couldn’t hit the broad side of a barn.

I tried to speak, but the sandy roast beef was pushing my tongue back and forcing my teeth apart.

“Guuh.”

“What’s that, son? I didn’t hear you.”

“Guuh.”

“How many times have I told you not to talk with your mouth full? You go on to your meeting, dear. This young gentleman is going to have to sit here until he finishes his roast beef.”

My father changed his shirt and left the house for his meeting without a word about the intriguing smell of cordite in his shirt drawer. The smell was probably stronger in my mind that it was in that drawer. I finally managed to swallow that bite of roast beef and the rest of my dinner. Freed from the table, I went up to listen to *The Thin Man* on the radio. No one ever found out how Mr. Johnson got shot asleep in his bed in the middle of a summer afternoon.

The Last Time I Saw Billy

Bobby and I were playing mumblety-peg with Bobby's new Barlow next to the hollyhocks under the cool of the big water maple tree in my backyard when Billy came striding up the walk from the back gate. It was late September but much too warm for the trench coat he was wearing. Billy didn't care. Ever since Casablanca played at the Shirley, Billy wore that trench coat everywhere. A cigarette hung from his lower lip. He removed it with his thumb and forefinger, cupping it in his palm, and exhaled through his teeth.

"Want a drag, punk?"

"No," said Bobby. "You know I don't smoke."

"I wasn't talking to you, punk. I was talking to Four-eyes there. What about it, Four-eyes?"

"Let's go back in the alley. My mom's in the house."

"Suits me. What say, Bobby? You comin' or are you gonna stand around playing with your jackknife?"

"I'm going home."

"OK, Bobby. Bobby-baby is goin' home, Four-eyes. Let's go burn some Luckies," snarled Billy as he led the way out the back gate into the alley.

We walked less than ten feet to the cover of the concrete block garage and squatted down on the soot-blackened gravel. Billy crushed the butt of his cigarette with his heel, pulled a fresh Lucky from his trench coat, then reached inside the coat and pulled a wooden kitchen match out of his shirt pocket. He held the match in his fist and struck it with his thumbnail.

With the impressive nonchalance of a veteran smoker, he swept the match to the end of the Lucky dangling from his lower lip. He took a deep drag and cupped the cigarette toward me.

"Here, punk. Have a coffin nail."

I took a puff. The hot acrid smoke closed the back of my throat. My eyes watered, and I started to cough.

"Geez, Four-eyes. Ain't you never smoked before? You got to breathe in natural-like."

My coughing stopped, and I tried again. This time I could feel the smoke burning in my chest.

"That's the way, punk. Now let it out slow-like."

"Here, Billy." I handed the cigarette back to him. "You finish it. I think I've had enough."

"Geez." Billy flicked the cigarette into the alley. "You spit all over it, punk. You're 'sposed to smoke the things, not eat 'em."

"Where did you get them, Billy?"

"Stole 'em from my old man. He was asleep on the porch when I was comin' out of the house. Took 'em right out of his pocket. Boy. He'd beat the shit outa me if he caught me."

"Yeh, I know. My fa ...old man spanks me sometimes."

"I don't mean spank, punk. I mean beat. Last week he came home drunk from down at Nielander's and nearly busted my ribs." Billy lit up another Lucky, leaned back against the garage, and blew the smoke in a hard stream toward the darkening sky.

"You mean he hit you?"

"You bet. One of these days I'll get him though, punk. One of these days I'll catch him."

"You mean you'd hit your father?"

"Hit him?" said Billy, jumping up. "If I get half a chance, I'll kill him."

"Sure you will, Billy," I said before I thought. He lashed out with his foot and caught me with the toe of his shoe right on the shin.

"Ow!"

"Don't you never call me a liar, punk," he yelled as he kicked again, catching me on the back of the thigh. "Never."

I cringed against the side of the garage. Billy glared down at me, spit contemptuously into the coal dust, then turned and stalked away with his hands in the pockets of his trench coat. That was the last time I ever saw Billy.

In spite of the sweet clover I chewed on my way to the house, my mother smelled the cigarette smoke, and when my father came home, I was whipped and sent to my room. I heard the sirens, and I could see the glow out my window, but my parents wouldn't let me go see the fire. Bobby saw the whole thing. He was there when the fireman found Billy's old man and took him bleeding and screaming to the hospital with a busted head. He even saw Billy in the back of the police car after they caught up with him hiding in the drainage ditch in the vacant lot up on McCoy Street with the hammer still in the pocket of his trench coat.

Later on, I traded a kid in my class six Red Menace bubble gum cards for a couple of Luckies and smoked them out behind the garage, but it wasn't the same without Billy.

Afterword

The time is a cool June evening in the mid-1970s. The place is a lodge on Lake Saranac in the Adirondacks. The occasion is a writers' conference sponsored by St. Lawrence University. The students—many of them—are from the Eastern universities or from New York City. Some of them have published in literary magazines; they are a sophisticated lot with a good background in modern literary criticism. That day, perhaps, they have been listening to Joyce Carol Oates, or Theodore Weiss of Princeton, or John Hawkes giving a complex talk on some aspect of writing. There has been considerable discussion of such writers as John Barth, Thomas Pynchon, John Ashbery, and Vladimir Nabokov.

They are here for an evening reading of some unpublished work. The fire is going in the big, stone fireplace. The lodge chairs are filled, and people are sitting on the floor, most of them with a beer in hand. And most of them are a little skeptical when a young man with a short blond beard and a manuscript under his arm steps up to the lectern. This had better be good. It had better come up to the Saranac standard of high seriousness. The talk dies off and James Perkins begins to read his fiction.

The first thing they notice is an accent unfamiliar on the Eastern ear—it's a border-state voice with something of the mountain South in it and the nearest thing they can recall is the country-western voice. It's not the Princeton or Brown or Bennington kind of voice they've been used to. But it has an easy charm. Sort of rustic, they think, but they listen a little harder as Jim takes them into his story.

Suddenly, before they know what has happened, they are laughing hard—a natural kind of laughter that doesn't come from literary subtleties or ingenious satire. They are laughing at a scene of Daddy and Pap and Uncle Eddie forking simultaneously for the last chicken gizzard on the platter or at the spectacle of six tail-coated pallbearers ramming the coffin containing Col. R. C. Jorgansen through the machinery shed door in an effort to put out a fire. The sophisticated preconceptions are forgotten. By gosh, here's a story—and a very funny one, too.

Jim takes them back into a childhood that can't have been more than some thirty years ago—but it sounds like something out of the timeless American past of all country childhoods. It has a touch of *Huckleberry Finn* in it, a touch of *Penrod and Sam*, a touch of *Peck's Bad Boy*, but there are a very real Bobby and Billy and Jim in it, even though they may be first cousins to Tom and Huck. Jim tells them about simple things—but the enormous adventures of boyhood—breaking the ice on the pond one winter morning and sharing a drink with a big raccoon, kid badmen trying to repeat the great train robbery by blowing up the streetcar with cap-pistol caps, stealing a pickle from the free lunch in the saloon, sliding down Cinder Hill one snowy day on a sled, and Halloween jokers tearing down a stone wall and getting caught at it.

It takes them back—even if they were brought up on East Sixty-ninth Street and have graduated from Miss Finch's and Sarah Lawrence, it takes them back. They are right there with Bobby and Billy and Jimmy waiting to make the big raid on the trolley car.

And they love it. This is the old, primeval scene when fiction first came into this world. The forest around, a big fire lighting up the clearing, people sitting on the ground completely seduced by a good story. And then...and then...What happens next?

Jim Perkins' stories make you want to know what happens next, make you want to be astonished by the laugh that lurks around the corner of the next paragraph. And when he's finished, the listeners are very sorry that it's over. I can't think of anything better to say about a book of fiction—I was sorry when this one was over.

Robie Macauley

About the Author

James Ashbrook Perkins, Professor in the Department of English at Westminster College, New Wilmington, PA, holds a B.A. from Centre College of Kentucky, an M.A. from Miami University, and a Ph.D. from the University of Tennessee.

Although his major interest lies in writing poetry, he has written scripts for radio, television, and film, published several short stories, and tried his hand at what he feels is the dullest form of prose, the scholarly article.

In 1971 he was awarded the Mississippi Arts Festival Senior Poetry Award for his series "Maps and Highways," and in 1975 and 1976 he was named Canaras Fellow in Poetry for the fiction international/St. Lawrence University Writers' Conference. In 1988 he won a Matrix Award for his editorial "Skipping Stones with Quiet Determination." He is a member of the National Writers Union and a former member of the United Steel Workers of America.

Since 1976 Perkins has been awarded three summer fellowships and participated in two summer institutes sponsored by the National Endowment for the Humanities. And in 1998 he was a Fulbright Visiting Professor at Seoul National University in Seoul, Korea.

Perkins has had seven other books published: *The Amish: 2 Perceptions* (1976)*; Billy-the-Kid, Chicken Gizzards and Other Tales* (1977); *The Woodcarver* (1978); *The Amish: 2 Perceptions 2* (1981); *Snakes, Butterbeans, and the Discovery of Electricity* (1990); *Southern Writers at Century's End*, which he edited with Jeffrey Folks (1997); *Robert Penn Warren's All the King's Men: Three Stage Versions*, which he edited with James A. Grimshaw, Jr. (2000); *For the Record: A Robert Drake Reader*, which he edited with Randy Hendricks (2001); and *Brother Enemy: Poems of the Korean War*, a translation on which he collaborated with Suh, Ji-moon (2002). In addition, his stories, poetry, and essays have appeared in more than 100 journals including: *The Antigonish Review*, *NYO*, *Story Quarterly*, *Fiction International*, *The Hiram Poetry Review*, *The Black Fly Review*, *Colorado Review*, *US 1 Worksheets*, and *The Cape Rock*.

Perkins has finished a novel, the further adventures of Four-eyes, titled "Plea-bargaining with Puberty." He is now at work on a collection of stranger short stories with the working title "A Thunderous Number of Weird."

Robie Macauley, who was on the editorial board of *Story* magazine, taught writing at Emerson College and Harvard University. Macauley served as editor of *The Kenyon Review*, fiction editor for *Playboy*, and as Executive Editor for Houghton Mifflin.

He was the author of two novels *Disguises of Love* and *A Secret History of Time to Come*, a collection of short stories *The End of Pity*, and a textbook for creative writing, *Technique in Fiction* (with George Lanning).

His stories frequently appeared in the *Best American Short Stories* and *O. Henry Prize Stories* anthologies and in magazines such as *Esquire*, *Playboy*, and *Cosmopolitan*; and his reviews and articles in *Vogue*, *Saturday Review*, and *The New York Times Book Review*. He was a fiction judge for the National Book Awards and a recipient of Fulbright, Rockefeller, and Guggenheim fellowships. Robie Macauley died in 1995.

William J. McTaggart is a professor emeritus of English at Westminster College. He is the author of *What Happens in Fort Lauderdale* which he wrote pseudonymously with the poet

William Heyen and *Winning: 100 Years of Westminster College Football.* He loves baseball and children and dogs and ducks. He remembers fondly the taste of Sunday dinners at his grandmother's house, where just about everything on the table was homegrown and homemade. He wrote the introduction for this book.

Nelson Oestreich, who did the illustrations that appear in this book, lives in New Wilmington, PA. He holds B.S. and M.F.A. degrees from Bowling Green State University and an M.A. from Kent State University.

Although he concentrates on woodcuts, Oestreich is a versatile artist who sculpts in both wood and metal and paints in acrylics, oils, and watercolors. Recently he has turned his attention to highly decorated, functional wood constructions and huge whimsical carved wooden heads.

During the past forty years he has exhibited in over 100 local, regional, and national exhibitions, and he has collected many awards. His work may be found in many public and private collections, including the Butler Institute of American Art, Bowling Green State University, The Hoyt Institute of Fine Arts, the Massillon Museum, and Westminster College. His prints have been reproduced in a number of magazines, and he has collaborated with the author of this book to produce *The Amish: 2 Perceptions*; *The Woodcarver*, *Billy-the-Kid, Chicken Gizzards, and Other Tales*; *The Amish: 2 Perceptions 2*; and the 1990 version of *Snakes, Butterbeans, and the Discovery of Electricity*. On his own, he wrote and illustrated *Amish Children: What they Learn*.

www.ingramcontent.com/pod-product-compliance
Lightning Source LLC
Chambersburg PA
CBHW030412310726
48979CB00002B/386

* 9 7 8 0 8 6 5 5 4 8 1 4 5 *